The SCANDAL ANNUAL 1·9·8·8

the SCANDAL ANNUAL 1·9·8·8

THE PARAGON PROJECT

PaperJacks LTD.

TORONTO   NEW YORK

AN ORIGINAL

SCANDAL ANNUAL 1988

PaperJacks LTD.
330 STEELCASE RD. E., MARKHAM, ONT. L3R 2M1
210 FIFTH AVE., NEW YORK, N.Y. 10010

First edition published February 1988

This original PaperJacks edition is printed from brand-new plates made from newly set, clear, easy-to-read type. No part of this book may be reproduced or transmitted in any form or by any means, electronic or mechanical, including photography, recording, or any information storage or retrieval system, without permission in writing from the publisher.

ISBN 0-7701-0762-1
Copyright © 1988 by Tom Biracree
All rights reserved
Printed in the USA

Dedication

To Nancy, whose love and patience sustained this project, even though 37,464 lbs of newspaper cluttered her home.

Acknowledgements

To the Cat in the Hat, Winnie the Pooh, Puff the Magic Dragon, Mickey Mouse, Chippendale, Dumbo, Pinnochio, Dinosaurs real and pretend, and all twenty-six letters of the alphabet—we couldn't have found the time to complete this book without you, guys.

CONTENTS

FOREWORD: *THE YEAR IN SCANDAL* — 1

CHAPTER 1: *SCANDALOUS QUOTES OF 1987:* The most outrageous and hilarious statements and misstatements of the year. — 9

CHAPTER 2: *NOW, THAT'S A CRIME:* Scandalous crimes, criminals, and stories about the good guys and bad guys of 1987. — 43

CHAPTER 3: *AMONG THE THINGS YOU DIDN'T WANT TO KNOW* . . . All the stories you wish you hadn't read about last year. — 79

CHAPTER 4: *WHAT A WAY TO GO:* The strangest deaths of 1987. — 113

CHAPTER 5: *IF YOU THINK YOU'VE GOT TROUBLES* . . . Just plain bad luck that plunged unfortunates into scandal.

CHAPTER 6:	*SCANDAL AROUND THE U.S.A.:* An All-American guided tour to misdoings in towns big and small.	149
CHAPTER 7:	*SCANDAL AROUND THE WORLD:* The juiciest international scandals of the year.	193
CHAPTER 8:	*BOY, THAT'S DUMB:* A look at exactly how stupid people were in 1987, along with the con games people tried to put over on you.	213
CHAPTER 9:	*THE TRULY BIZARRE SCANDALS OF 1987:* The strangest of the strange last year.	239
CHAPTER 10:	*EVERY DAY, IN AMERICA...* Ever wonder what scandals are taking place around you right now? A guide to the misbehavior of everyday life.	263
CHAPTER 11:	*THE EXCLUSIVE SCANDAL ANNUAL SINDEX:* Americans rank sins from murder to misdemeanors to produce our exclusive scandal rating system, which you can apply to your friends' behavior.	269
AFTERWORD:	*A LOOK AHEAD TO SCANDAL IN 1988*	277

FOREWORD
THE YEAR IN SCANDAL

THANK YOU, JIM. Thank you, Tammy. Thank you, Ollie, Fawn, and the Ayatollah, you old devil you. And more thanks to Gary and Donna and Oral and Sean and all the guys on Wall Street. Thanks for producing those scandals that filled the headlines throughout most of 1987.

It's no secret that last year was the best year for headline scandals since the Watergate era. The Iran-Contra affair provided a delicious mix of international intrigue and domestic political skulduggery. The Gary Hart affair added a welcome interlude of sex and power. The PTL scandal provided a wonderful mixture of kinky sex, religion, and greed. We at the Paragon Project hope you enjoyed watching the news as much as we did.

But we didn't spend all our time just poring over the headlines. We also combed tens of thousands of news reports to find a host of shocking, bizarre, outrageous, and just plain funny scandals you might not have read about last year. Through our detective work, we found every kind of misbehavior from high crimes to low-down rudeness, involving everyone from world-famous celebrities to the people next door.

THE YEAR IN SCANDAL

The Scandal Annual—1987, America's almanac of impropriety, presents even more delicious dirt than did last year's book, which entertained hundreds of thousands of readers all over the world. You'll find scandals involving everyone from the queen of England to a dog in Rochester, New York, in locations ranging from America's big cities to the mountains of Tibet. If the experiences of last year's readers are any indication, you'll find this book a storehouse of entertaining anecdotes that will make you the life of the party for weeks.

Before we get to all the juicy details of 1987's scandals, we thought we'd provide a fun little quiz that serves as a taste of what's inside:

1. In what publication did this advice appear: "If you do get busted, don't panic. You will be out in several hours"?

   a. The National Security Council employee manual

   b. A manual of job descriptions used by Wall Street investment banking firms

   c. An instruction manual issued to a gang of seventy-five Brooklyn teenagers who ride buses to shoplift at suburban malls

2. Who said, "He had the right sliminess"?

   a. The leader of the "Bring Back **Gary Hart**" campaign

   b. The leader of the "Bring Back **Jim Bakker**" campaign

   c. The ad executive who cast actor **David Leisure** in Isuzu's "liar" commercials

3. What religious leader reportedly cries when he's frustrated, pulls people's hair, and wears disposable diapers?

   a. the **Ayatollah Khomeini**
   b. **Pope John Paul II**
   c. Two-year-old **Osel Torres,** the newest Lama Yeshe, named a Tibetan Buddhist holy man by the Dalai Lama

4. Who said, "I like to went into shock"?

   a. **Jimmy Carter**, when he heard that his daughter **Amy** had flunked out of college
   b. **Peter Holm**, when told he might have to scrimp by on less than $80,000 a month alimony from **Joan Collins**
   c. A Jackson, Mississippi, businessman who was told by police that the prostitute with whom he'd been partying was a transvestite and a carrier of AIDS

5. Who said, "We're just normal, friendly people not doing anything strange, except we do it in the nude"?

   a. **Hugh Hefner**
   b. The cast of **Oh! Calcutta!**
   c. **Ellyn Kern**, spokesperson for National Nude Weekend, sponsored by nudist camps across the country

THE YEAR IN SCANDAL

6. To whom does this quote refer: "His mind works, but only when he cares to use it"?

    a. Frankenstein's monster

    b. **Max Headroom**

    c. **Ronald Reagan**

7. Who said, "We are not looking for fear. We are not looking for love. We are looking for respect"?

    a. The commander of U.S. naval forces in the Persian Gulf

    b. The coach of the New York Giants

    c. The commissioner of the IRS, telling Congress there's no need to pass a "taxpayers' bill of rights" to govern the conduct of IRS agents

8. Who was Federal Agent **Robert Stutman** talking about when he said, "Usually we're trying to catch people who are trying to beat the system. These people *were* the system"?

    a. The staff of the National Security Council

    b. The Association of Television Evangelists

    c. A huge drug-smuggling organization run by Pan Am passenger-service workers at JFK Airport in New York

9. Who said **this** about his own speaking ability: "If they can teach Mr. Ed, they can teach me"?

THE YEAR IN SCANDAL

   a. **Mike the Dog**, who starred in *Down and Out in Beverly Hills*

   b. **Sean Penn**

   c. **Bruce Babbitt**, Democratic presidential candidate

10. Who said, "Hello, gorgeous. Could we discuss the possibility of rape?"

   a. **Nancy Reagan**, to **Mr. T**

   b. **Bruce Willis** to **Cybil Shepherd**

   c. **Joan Baez**, to *Miami Vice* star **Don Johnson**

11. Who said, "The decision went beyond dumb and reached all the way to stupid"?

   a. **Madonna**, on why she married **Sean Penn**

   b. A Warner Brothers executive, on the decision to make the **Madonna** film *Who's That Girl?*

   c. **Lee Iacocca**, on Chrysler's selling as new cars that had been damaged in testing

12. Who said, "Just remember you are God, and act accordingly"?

   a. **President Reagan**, to **Ollie North**

   b. **Mrs. Roberts**, to her husband **Oral**

   c. **Shirley MacLaine**, in her seminar called Connecting with the Higher Self

Did you recognize any of those quotations? Even if you didn't, you probably figured out that the answer to all twelve questions was C.

But enough hard mental work. It's time to lean back and enjoy the wonderful reading ahead of you in *The Scandal Annual—1987*.

CATHEDRAL RAMPAGE

New Orleans, June 24

The Rev. Gerald Barrett and police Sgt. Robert Williams, right, check damage to holy water fonts that police said were smashed by a man on a rampage Tuesday in historic St. Louis Cathedral.

1.
SCANDALOUS QUOTES OF 1987

A LOT OF THE VERY BEST in scandalous entertainment in any year is provided not by what people do but what they say. That's especially true of those who often speak in public: America's famous actors, politicians, executives, and other celebrities. Those celebrated mouths were especially witty in 1987. For example, when accepting his People's Choice Award for Favorite TV Game Show Host, **Pat Sajack** said: "I'd like to take you back quite a few years now to a small middle-class home where a little boy was growing up with a dream that he might one day make a lot of people happy by giving away millions of dollars in cash and prizes, maybe work with a beautiful blond young lady, and maybe get a little recognition for himself. And of course that little boy grew up to be Lieutenant Colonel Oliver North."

Other celebrity quotes reveal the less attractive side of people in the news. For example, actor **Dennis Hopper** related a conversation he had with his wife, **Michelle Phillips**, when she was about to leave him after eight days of marriage: "I said, 'Well, what am I going to do?' . . . And she said, 'Have you ever thought about suicide?'"

Occasionally a celebrity will get caught with his foot in

his mouth. For example, shortly before he announced his engagement to **Alex Maas**, **Johnny Carson** was asked if he planned to marry again. His reply: "When the Ayatollah appears in *Playgirl*."

In the following pages, you'll find well over a hundred scandalous quotes from 1987. After you've finished reading, you'll understand why a lot of embarrassed celebrities feel like **Andy MacPhail**, a vice president of the Minnesota Twins, commenting after he'd failed to sign a star pitcher: "I'm going to be a household word, like 'toilet.'"

❝

"Is there one law for soap-opera actresses and another for the homeless? Be fair. Peter helped you get rich. Give Holm a decent home."—**Peter Holm**, picketing **Joan Collins**'s house in support of his claim to be paid $16,500 a month so he could rent a "decent" home.

❝

"Let me give him his due; he would have made a hell of a king."—former House Speaker **Tip O'Neill**, on **Ronald Reagan**.

❝

"That girl knew exactly why she was going down there. Besides, it only lasted fifteen minutes."—**Tammy Faye**

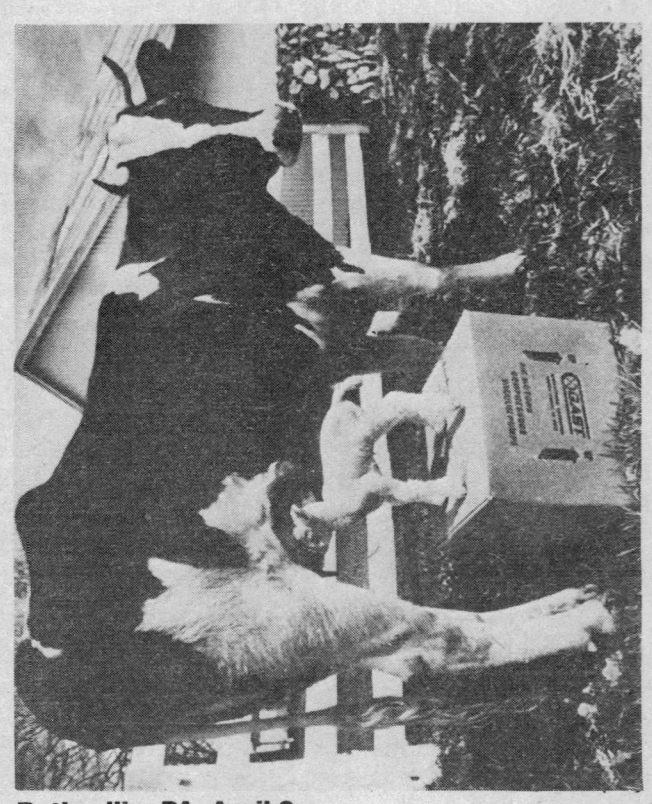

Rothsville, PA, April 9
This baby lamb, one of a set of triplets born on Sheryl Wenger's farm, was rejected by its mother. But it found nourishment at a teat of a three-year-old Holstein heifer named Becky, who was born without female reproductive organs but with the ability to milk. (Roxanne L. Platt)

Bakker, on **Jessica Hahn**, whom she refers to as her husband's "affairette."

❝

"I was greatly affected by that wonderful evening, for it was the first time I had fallen in love."—**Peter Holm**, in court papers, recalling his first date with **Joan Collins**.

❝

"I have met many movie stars, and they always say, 'Let's have lunch.' And it never happens. So when he rang, I was surprised."—**Marc Christian**, on how he met **Rock Hudson**, who became his lover.

❝

"You could fit everything I've learned about men on the head of a pin and still have room left for the Lord's Prayer."—**Cher**.

❝

"I get very chemically unbalanced when I get nervous. I either get hives or start twitching."—**Daryl Hannah**, who got hives in her nude scene in the movie, *Reckless*.

On the sale of arms to Iran, South Dakota **Governor William Janklow** said, "The only way we want to give arms to Iran is by dropping them from the bay of a B-1 bomber."

"When you're in the desert and you're dying of thirst, you don't ask if the water they are giving you is Schweppes or Perrier."—Contra leader **Adolfo Calero**, on his lack of curiosity about the sources of his funding.

DOES THIS PROMOTE DEVIL WORSHIP?

The following is a passage from a home economics textbook that an Alabama federal judge agreed was anti-Christian and promoted "secular humanism": "When you recognize that you are the one in charge of your life, you will be way ahead of where you would be if you think of your life as something that just happens to you."

LIKE WHEN YOU'RE DRIVING DOWN THE FREEWAY IN L.A.?

"We also offer automatic fire extinguishers for those times when, you know, someone throws a Molotov cocktail into your car."—Bob Schatz, sales clerk at a shop selling anti-terrorist equipment.

NOBODY SAYS IT BETTER

George Burns summed up the year this way: "It was a great year for me. I started it. I finished it."

THOSE COMMIES JUST DON'T KNOW HOW TO BOOGIE

Announcer to the audience at a Moscow rock concert: "You can display more emotion if you want. Rock back and forth in your seats."

JUST TO REASSURE YOU AIRLINE TRAVELERS ...

Harvard Medical School researcher Martin C. Moore-Eng made this comment following the revelation that airline pilots sometimes fall asleep during long flights:

"When you're in the cabin and your head is rolling over and you can't stay awake, just remember the guy up front is human, too."

"This morning, I had planned to clear up U.S.-Soviet differences on intermediate-range missiles, but I decided to clean out Ronny's sock drawer instead."—First Lady **Nancy Reagan**, joking about her reputation as the power behind the scenes at the White House.

"The routine promotion of condoms through advertising has been stopped by networks who are so hypocritically priggish that they refuse to describe disease control as they promote disease transmission." —Representative **Henry Waxman** of California, condemning network television executives for banning commercials for condoms, which help prevent the transmission of AIDS, while running programs that often emphasize casual sex.

THE SEND-PHIL-DONAHUE-TO-AFGHANISTAN FUND

Said **Phil Donahue**, who broadcast his television show from the Soviet Union for a week: "I believe we can trust the Russians."

THE SELF-APPOINTED MARTYR AWARD...

Goes to Jonathan Jay Pollard, who was convicted and sentenced for selling American secrets to Israel. Evidently comparing the U.S. government to that of Nazi Germany, he said: "Anne and I feel as if we're aboard one of those cattle cars pulling up to the separation platform at Auschwitz, while all about us the Jewish community just sits like mute spectators awaiting the fall of the ax."

"My doctors told me this morning my blood pressure was so low that I can start reading the newspapers." —**President Reagan**, after prostate surgery.

"We rebuke this virus and we command your immune system to function in the name of Jesus."—**Pat Robertson**, attempting to heal an AIDS victim on *700 Club*, his TV show.

"It [the United States] is an important country and our largest contributor, so we have to take into account its sensitivities and preoccupations."—a United Nations official, on why a U.N. film about the homeless would include no footage from the United States.

"A lot of its readers are of an age where they forget to cancel."—ad executive **Jerry Della Femina**, on why *Reader's Digest* has such a large circulation.

"The press is like the peculiar uncle you keep in the attic—just one of those unfortunate things."—Watergate conspirator **G. Gordon Liddy**.

A MODERN MORAL DILEMMA

"In a way, I want the dealers busted because they're sleazy characters. But they're selling me good stuff."—a

New York University student, on drug dealers who infest a park near the school.

"You get in bed and wind your legs around and everyone has a fine time. And all you need to do to see how ridiculous it is to have a mirror in the room." —novelist **Mary Lee Settle**, on graphic depictions of sex in fiction.

"It makes you wonder what they're smoking at the Tobacco Institute."—New York Congressman **Charles E. Schumer**, replying to a charge by the Tobacco Institute that a proposal to ban smoking in public buildings was based on "personal and political agenda rather than scientific fact."

"Tell them they've got the wrong place."—a White House press officer, to a receptionist announcing a phone call from *Success* magazine.

"For six years, we went around saying that **Ronald Reagan** didn't know what was going on. And now when he says the same thing about himself, we say he's lying."—Speaker of the House **Jim Wright**, a Democrat.

AH, THE OLD FASHIONED JOYS OF TOILET CLEANING...

Said **Jessica Hahn**, about her one-night stand with evangelist **Jim Bakker**: "I yearn to have my childlike faith back. I wish I was fourteen years old and cleaning toilets again. I used to sing; I was happy."

Imelda Marcos on her "hidden wealth": "You can search the deepest and darkest vaults in Switzerland, you can comb the length and breadth of the United States, and you can dig up all 7,100 islands of the Philippines, but you won't find it. Only **Ferdinand** and I know where the hidden wealth is deposited."

UNDERSTATEMENT OF THE YEAR

"If I could have planned his weekend... I would have scheduled it differently."—**Lee Hart**, wife of **Gary**

Hart, on the weekend when her husband was caught in his town house with **Donna Rice**.

Said **Steve Farr**, Kansas City Royals relief pitcher, when asked whether his recent injury could be partly mental: "How could it be? I don't have a college education."

FILM REVIEW OF THE YEAR

New York *Daily News* critic **Alan Carter**, on the film *Ernest Goes to Camp*: "How best to describe this aggressively unfunny mess? Ever walk in something unpleasant and trail the smell with you for blocks? In this film, the smell never seems to go away."

"I wasn't interested in it going for chocolate bars or soda pops. I wanted something to kill the Commies." —retired mining executive E. Thomas Clagette on the money he contributed to the Contras.

"What do you do when your wife wakes up in the middle of the night, night after night, and asks, 'Do you think he suffered a lot?'"—Martin Levin, after Billionaire Boys Club founder **Joe Hunt** was sentenced to life in prison for killing the Levins' son Ron.

AT HIS AGE, HE'S BOUND TO BE NONCHALANT

New York State Supreme Court Judge **Abraham Levy**, eighty-two, after a woman barged into his office, announced she was going to kill him, and fired two shots, missing him both times: "It's all in a day's work."

"Snow White has to cook and clean for seven guys who aren't even that attractive, and she's waiting around for somebody to kiss her. She's got trouble, real trouble."—author **Tama Janowitz**, on the fiftieth anniversary of the motion picture, *Snow White*.

"I think a woman ought to stay sexy for her husband. She ought to dress sexy and keep herself exciting. I still flirt a lot with my husband at home."—**Tammy Faye Bakker**, as quoted in a book on the wives of evangelists.

Evidently, the interview took place before the sex scandal involving her husband hit the papers.

"The real problem at PTL was prosperity theology . . . that God is the holy slot machine. You put in $10, you get out $20."—the Reverend **Jerry Falwell**.

"She has a great deal of love for God, but she felt that *Playboy* could best report her story."—lawyer Dominic Barbara, announcing that **Jessica Hahn** would tell her story in one of this country's least religious magazines. Surely the large fee she received from *Playboy* played no part in her decision.

AND WHAT WAS BARBARA'S REPLY?

When asked by **Barbara Walters** if it was true that **Gary Hart** had promised to divorce his wife and marry her, **Donna Rice** asked, "You think I'm a moron?"

"It was too little too late. Apparently, old age caught up with him. He was at minimum ten years old."

—Florida Audubon Society ornithologist, on the death of Orange Band, the last of the world's dusky seaside sparrows.

"It was pop, pop, pop, like the Fourth of July ... twenty-five to thirty shots in just a few seconds. There were people dead on the sidewalk."—a restaurant owner describing the shooting spree during which a gunman killed six people and wounded fourteen in two Palm Bay, Florida, shopping centers.

"I'm thinking ... I'm thinking"—**Nancy Reagan**, when asked to say a few kind words about the press.

"How many criminals can claim 56,000 victims?" —the judge who sentenced banker **Marvin Warner** to 3.5 years in prison and a $22 million fine for his role in the collapse of the Columbus, Ohio, Home State Savings.

"Of course there is no need for a death penalty in a civilized society—but first get your civilized society." —**Sir Ian Percival**, speaking before the British Parliament in defense of his proposal to restore the death penalty.

TAKE THAT, YOU COMMIE PINKOS!

Said *Conservative Digest* publisher **William Kennedy**: "**President Reagan** has been trying to keep the Russians out of Nicaragua and the Middle East. Only a pack of liberal wimps and Moscow Ballet lovers would consider that a hanging offense."

"Wesley [John Wesley, founder of the Methodist church] believed in earning all you can, saving all you can, to give all you can. But not to tailbacks."—a Southern Methodist University professor, after the NCAA banned football at SMU for a year because the school was caught giving illegal payments to players.

CAMPAIGN RHETORIC

"He says he needs four more years to finish his job. That's to bomb the other half of the city."—former Philadelphia Mayor **Frank Rizzo,** in his campaign to unseat Mayor **Wilson Goode,** who Rizzo alleges was responsible for an attack on a house held by radicals, which resulted in eleven deaths and the burning of sixty-one homes.

"If I believe . . . some of the articles I read, I'd fear for my safety here right now, because I'm sitting with seven other bishops who have nothing in mind but to assault me sexually."—New York's **John Cardinal O'Connor,** on stories about priests and sex, following reports that some priests have contracted AIDS.

"He is as heroic as **Charles Manson** and as much of a mountain man as **Liberace.**"—Author **Jack Olsen,** on much-publicized killer **Claude Dallas, Jr.,** who was arrested a year after he escaped from an Idaho prison.

DO AS I SAY, NOT AS I DO

President Reagan, talking to schoolchildren, said, "It sort of settled down to trading arms for hostages, and that's a little like paying ransom to a kidnapper. If you do it, the kidnapper's encouraged to go kidnap someone else."

New York Mets outfielder **Lenny Dykstra,** on the religious conversion of former teammate **Kevin Mitchell:** "Mitch found God in spring training. Then, every night, he'd try to find a goddess."

"The Consumer Product Safety Commission wants to wait until it has a pile of dead babies."—activist **Ann Brown,** urging the commission to ban dangerous baby pacifiers.

LOOKING ON THE BRIGHT SIDE

Said former Chief Justice of the California Supreme Court, **Rose Bird:** "Ours is an amphetamine society, without the stability of an anchor, hurtling from one idea to another, momentarily clinging to them for support, but then discarding them."

"Florida has more physicians per capita than any state. Florida also has more lawyers per capita than most states."—the head of the Academy of Florida Trial Lawyers, on the state's malpractice problem.

AND WHO DO YOU SUPPOSE UNCLOTHES THEM?

Tammy Faye Bakker said, "I wear them and give them away. I have clothed many, many ladies."

NOTHING LIKE A PICNIC BY THE OLD MISSILE SILO

An ad for Rockwell International proclaimed, "Like Yosemite National Park, Tactical Weapons Systems are a national resource."

"You've got to look on the bright side. This is the best liver so far."—the father of a seven-month-old girl who had just received her fourth liver transplant.

"I guess we'll see how funny she is in a court of law."—the lawyer for **Victoria Principal,** who filed a $3 million lawsuit after **Joan Rivers** broadcast Principal's unlisted telephone number on her late-night TV show.

"Aw, give me a hundred years and get it over with." —convicted Mafia underboss **Salvatore "Tom Mix" Santoro,** age seventy-two, urging the judge to hurry up and sentence him. The judge obliged.

"Kemo sábe, these Texas Rangers are good men." —*Lone Ranger* actor **Clayton Moore,** after Texas Rangers recovered a silver-plated six-shooter that had been stolen from his luggage.

No doubt the Ayatollah was impressed by this inscription in the Bible **President Reagan** sent to Iran when trying to arrange the arms-for-hostages swap: "And the Scripture, foreseeing that God would justify the gentiles by faith, preached the Gospel beforehand to Abraham, saying, 'All the nations shall be blessed in you.'" —Galatians 3:8.

"We can also sell refrigerators to Eskimos and carry coal to Newcastle."—Soviet Foreign Ministry spokesman, reporting that the Soviet Union had given a Russian-made streetcar to the city of San Francisco.

"I gave her life, I can take her life away."—surrogate mother **Mary Beth Whitehead,** in a tape-recorded threat played at the trial in which she lost custody of **Baby M.**

"Women often throw their panties at me when I speak. It happened again just yesterday. I just don't know what got into Senator Mikulski."—Senator **Pete Domenici** of New Mexico, during an off-the-record speech at an all-male club. The comment somehow got back to Senator **Barbara Mikulski** of Maryland, who demanded and got an apology.

"Lady Liberty says at her base, 'Give me your tired, your poor, your huddled masses.' She doesn't ask for a dollar."—Senator **Bill Bradley** of New Jersey, who introduced legislation to repeal a law allowing the National Park Service to charge a dollar to visit the Statue of Liberty.

"I called up the movie academy and said if I didn't get an Oscar, God was calling me home. They said, 'Have a nice trip.'"—**Bob Hope,** after **Oral Roberts** claimed that God had told him he would die if he didn't raise $8 million.

"I don't know why the people of Toledo need better access to an amusement park when they can come to Washington and watch some of the world's biggest clowns for free."—Senator **Gordon Humphrey** of New Hampshire, commenting on a $87.5 billion highway bill loaded with special interest appropriations, such as building a highway that would make it faster for people in Toledo to drive to an amusement park.

"Anyone who can't make a profit by borrowing money at 5.8 percent and lending it at 13.8 percent should find another line of work."—Congressman **Frank Annunzio,** refuting claims by the banking industry that a bill limiting credit card interest rates would ruin them financially.

"I'm like a land mine on those—four guests in one. You get celebrity child, rock-star ex-wife, former drug addict, and movie star."—**Carrie Fisher,** on the talk show circuit.

Boy George, on his much-publicized breakup with **Jon Moss:** "I'm not embarrassed about it. If he was ugly, it might have embarrassed me, but he's cute."

"I remember calling one agent and saying, 'This is Elinor Donohue,' and the agent said, 'Who are you trying to kid? She'd dead.'"—**Elinor Donohue,** former *Father Knows Best* star, on her return to show business.

"I'd mind if it [my skull] ended up on a shelf in an ambiguous way. I think I would like to have my name on it."—**Debbie Harry,** on her anonymous skull collection.

THE DUKE BLASTS REAGAN

John Wayne, always a straight shooter, was never shy about expressing his opinions, even to a friend like **Ronald Reagan.** In a letter discovered this year, the Duke blasted Reagan for having written a fund-raising letter that Wayne believed contained false statements about the Panama Canal treaty. Wayne's letter read, in part, "I'll show you point by God damn point where you are misleading people. [If you persist in making] erroneous remarks, someone will publicize your letter to prove that you are not as thorough on your reviewing of this treaty as you say, or are damned obtuse when it comes to reading the English language."

Television evangelist **Jimmy Swaggart** once advised his audience: "Don't ever bargain with Jesus. He's a Jew."

"If you look on heaven's scenes, you'll find the streets are guarded by United States Marines."—Marine Major General **Carl Mundy,** resorting to a paraphrase of the Marine Hymn when grilled by a House committee on the scandals involving U.S. Marine embassy guards.

WHAT PLANET IS THIS MAN LIVING ON?

"These are good times to be a Republican."—Vice President **George Bush,** as quoted in the middle of the Iran-Contra scandal.

IN THE CONFIDENCE-IN-OUR LEADERSHIP DEPARTMENT...

After **Ronald Reagan** confused him with **Lee Iacocca**, New York Governor **Mario Cuomo** remarked, "I guess we all look alike."

"She's just the kind of person Wellesley is usually proud of. She is young, imaginative, a successful entrepreneur, and she was trying to share her experiences with other women."—a Wellesley College professor, talking about Wellesley trustee Henrietta Holsman, who told a college audience that Hispanic workers at her L.A. firm were lazy and that it was hard to keep black workers from going back on the street to deal drugs.

"It sells so good I'm thinking about putting '538' on every room on the fifth floor."—the manager of the Sheraton Sand Key in Clearwater, Florida, on the flood of reservation requests for the hotel room in which **Jim Bakker** had his sexual encounter with **Jessica Hahn**.

"In a way we taught them everything they know, but we didn't teach them everything we knew."—**A. W. Clausen,** chief executive of BankAmerica, on a takeover bid by another company run by many ex-BankAmerica employees.

MORE CLEAR THINKING FROM THE VICE PRESIDENT

George Bush, on how he would have handled the Iran-Contra affair:—"I probably would have done the same things differently that the President would have done differently."

A stockholder at the annual meeting of the *Washington Post* asked the publisher, "Have you ever committed adultery?" The publisher, **Donald Graham,** replied: "No. And at the directors' meeting this morning, we voted that you could only ask that question of one director."

IS SHE A SECRETARY OR SECRETARY OF STATE?

Fawn Hall, Oliver North's secretary, pontificated, "Sometimes you have to go above the written law."

"I like him. Have him stripped, washed, and brought to my tent."—**Cher,** upon seeing her much younger boyfriend, **Rob Cameletti,** for the first time in a New York nightclub.

JUST DRIPPING WITH SYMPATHY

Indiana University basketball coach **Bobby Knight,** talking to campers about the cocaine-induced death of former Maryland star **Len Bias:** "He wanted to be one of the boys. He wanted to be cool. Well, he was so cool, he's cold. He's as cold as heck."

IN THE UNDERSTATEMENT DEPARTMENT...

"I am a child of God, I err."—John Rye, former chairman of Lamb Technicon Corp. in Michigan, after being sentenced to three years in jail for not reporting a mere $1.3 million in income.

Playboy magazine asked **Ferdinand** and **Imelda Marcos,** "You think of yourselves as gods, then?"

IMELDA: Yes, because we are on a divine mission . . . to return to the Philippines to reclaim our destiny.

FERDINAND: We are part of the achievement of being a god. That is what we are about now. An ordinary mortal would not be able to stand it.

Tennis player **Ivan Lendl,** in response to **John McEnroe's** comment that playing on the same Davis Cup team as Lendl could be tough to swallow: "With his mouth, it's hard to imagine him having difficulty swallowing anything."

IN THE BAREFOOT-AND-PREGNANT DEPARTMENT . . .

Morman church president **Ezra Taft Benson** said in a TV broadcast that the divine role of women is "to conceive, to bear, to nourish, to love, and to train."

"Only two legitimate national holidays remain . . . holidays with a specific, naturally evolved meaning, the celebration of which we find refreshing and correct, and in the celebration of which we, as a People, are united. Those holidays are the Super Bowl and the Academy Awards."—Pulitzer Prize-winning playwright **David Mamet**.

Gloria Steinem, on **Geraldine Ferraro's** candidacy for Vice President: "What has the women's movement learned from her candidacy? Never get married."

"I wouldn't let my kid hear what I do on stage." —**Eddie Murphy**.

"I think I'll be profoundly wise and generous, liberal, understanding. I'd be surprised if I'd be less than perfect as a father."—**Woody Allen**, joking about impending fatherhood after it became known that his girlfriend, **Mia Farrow,** was pregnant.

"I'm one star away from **Dolly Parton. Raymond Massey** is between us. I hope we don't smother him." —**Bernadette Peters,** on getting her star on Hollywood's Walk of Fame.

"It's the longest job I've had since the Eleventh Air Force in World War II."—**Charlton Heston,** on the cancellation of the TV series, *The Colbys.*

"Bond's women were exhausting. And I got fed up with explosions and being blown up. I always thought they were trying to kill me so they could get out of paying me."—**Roger Moore,** on playing James Bond.

"And if he does run again, I'll be there. But I won't cook any more dinners."—**William Broadhurst,** the other man on the famous "Monkey Business" cruise with **Gary Hart** and **Donna Rice.**

"Politics is, for me, forgive and—as you may have heard—sometimes forget."—**Ronald Reagan.**

"You'd better ask the bitch."—Rolling Stones **Keith Richards,** when asked if he saw an end to the bitching between himself and **Mick Jagger.**

"I've got an IQ of 7."—**Barbara Stanwyck,** on the character she played on *The Colbys.*

Michelle Phillips, on the breakup of **The Mamas and the Papas:** "Don't get involved with a tenor—especially when your husband's the bass."

"The way I kiss, it wouldn't stop there."—**Loretta Young,** on the fact that she's been celibate for thirty-two years.

"Trust me, there's no one here who can answer your questions."—woman who answered the phone at a Wall Street firm after the cops busted nine employees who allegedly ran a cocaine ring.

"We may disagree on our effectiveness politically, but I'm a much better actor than he ever was."—**Susan Sarandon,** on **Ronald Reagan.**

"She's a sexy woman. She's a real good-lookin' old broad."—**Geraldo Rivera,** on **Barbara Walters.**

"I like short introductions, because for years mine was, 'Will the defendant please rise?'"—**G. Gordon Liddy,** former Watergate convict.

"I got what I deserved. I got beat and got a fat lip in the process."—Senator **John Warner** of Virginia, on playing squash with women on National Women in Sports Day.

"I don't have to do three-legged lesbian nuns." —**Geraldo Rivera,** claiming his new talk show will be different from **Phil Donahue's** and **Oprah Winfrey's.**

"I'm twenty-eight, my daughter is twenty-six, and soon she will pass me and be older."—**Zsa Zsa Gabor.**

General **Richard Secord,** on Lieutenant Colonel **Oliver North:** "He was like a mule—and you know how the army treats mules. You load him up and load him up until pretty soon his back breaks. Then you eat him."

2.
NOW, THAT'S A CRIME

THE CRIME STORY OF THE YEAR was the ultimate in human perversity, the absolute outer limits of shock and degradation. There is nothing worse that a human being can do to other human beings than what went on in the house at 3550 North Marshall Street in Philadelphia.

The monstrous story came into the open when a twenty-six-year-old woman named Josephina Rivera escaped from a car and flagged down police. Acting on her information, they got a search warrant for the Marshall Street house.

They discovered three half-naked young black women in chains in the basement, one of them huddled in a pit and covered with plywood and sandbags. Two of the women, both eighteen years old, had been in the house for months, during which time they were repeatedly raped, beaten, and tortured. They were fed dog food and had screwdrivers jammed into their ears when they were "bad." The third woman, twenty-four years old, had been in the house only two days.

This story of torture and sex slavery was only the beginning, however. In the refrigerator, police found white plastic bags containing twenty-four pounds of human body parts. According to Rivera and the other captives, the owner of the house, forty-three-year-old

Gary Michael Heidnik, had taken one captive named Sharon Linday, and "beat her with a stick and cuffed her to the ceiling beam and let her hang there.... All the captives were chained... and watched her hang until she died."

But that wasn't all. Rivera also said, "Heidnik carried Sandy's lifeless body from the basement to the first floor. Another thirty minutes passed, and Rivera heard an electric saw running upstairs and a foul smell coming from upstairs, as though someone was cooking something that had gone sour or bad.

"She was told by Heidnik that he killed Sandy and chopped her body up and put some of Sandy into a pot and cooked her up and fed her to the captives."

That still wasn't the end of the atrocities. Rivera led police to the body of another woman who, like all the captives, was a mentally deficient adult. This woman's nude body was found in a remote area of New Jersey; an autopsy revealed she had been electrocuted.

Rivera described her death: "Debbie was being punished for not doing what she was told and for being bad. After Debbie was forced into the hole, Heidnik filled it up with water from a garden hose and took a live electric cord and made me hold the live line on the handcuffs of Debbie while she stood in the hole.... Debbie kept screaming in pain as the electricity ran through her body."

The horrible tale ended when Heidnik took Rivera out to recruit yet another victim. Heidnik, who is white, was a self-proclaimed minister who had made a fortune investing in the stock market. It's hard to believe, however, that he wasn't Satan incarnate.

Heidnik may have been the worst criminal of 1987, but he was far from the only one. Many of the scandalous crime stories of last year are a lot less gruesome, and a lot more amusing. We hope you enjoy the following look at 1987 in crime.

PAWS ON PARADE

Keston, England, June 18

Minstrel, the resident cat at the Metropolitan Dog School in Keston, Kent, walks past a line-up of German Shepherd police dogs. The dogs are being trained at Keston for the Police Dog Championships at Imber Court, East Molesley, Surrey.

BAGELS MEAN LOCKS FOR EX-CON

Anthony Clarizio was thrown back into federal prison as a parole violator. His offense: eating too many bagels with poppy seeds while on parole.

That may sound strange until you understand that ingesting poppy seeds produces the same results from a urine test as does the use of heroin or any other drug that's a poppy derivative. Clarizio, who had served time for loan-sharking and extortion, claimed he never had a drug problem and that throwing him back in jail for bagel eating was ridiculous. The government countered that it was concerned that all inmates and parolees would use bagel eating as an excuse for failing their drug tests.

STEEPED IN TROUBLE

When Petty Officer Patricia Roach of the U.S. Navy tested positive for cocaine use after a random drug test, she provided a novel explanation. It seems that she bought a box of Health Inca Tea, a South American product that was supposedly made from "decocanized coca leaves." According to Roach, however, the illegal stuff was in fact still present in the brew. The petty officer was acquitted at her court martial. Then she filed a $6 million lawsuit against the makers of the tea, who probably think all the publicity is well worth the costs of defending the lawsuit.

TAKE-A-NUMBER TIME AT THE BANK

In San Leandro, California, two robbers happened to be standing in separate lines at the same branch of the Bank of America at the same time. One guy was in the express line, the other in a regular line, and at the same moment, both men flashed guns and demanded money. Cops are convinced it was a coincidence, but we'll see if "double dating" gets to be a trend.

THE SHY GUNMAN

It's tough to be shy, especially if your business is robbing hamburger stands. That's why a young gunman who approached the window of a drive-in restaurant in Stockton, California, got tongue-tied when he realized he'd left his demand note in the car. He walked away from the window, returned a few minutes later, and handed over a note that demanded money and cheeseburgers. He got $45, but left before his burgers were done.

MOST NOVEL LEGAL ARGUMENT OF THE YEAR

Richard A. Richards was sentenced to spend the rest of his "natural life" in jail for first-degree murder. Now he's suing the state for false imprisonment. His unique argument: he had a permanent pacemaker implanted surgically in January 1985, at which time his "natural" life was over. Since he would have died without the pacemaker, Richards claims he's now living an "artificial life." He's seeking immediate release, plus damages for false imprisonment.

YOU'D BETTER MAKE FIDO SIT DOWN BEFORE HE READS THIS

A judge in Rochester, New York, handed down a landmark decision, ruling that dogs are not American citizens and thus are not entitled to file lawsuits. The decision stunned Mr. and Mrs. Carl Feinstock, who were incensed when their dog Ari, whom they refer to as their "baby," was accidently left off a flight by U.S. Air baggage handlers in Florida. Ari's suit for damages for ill-treatment was thrown out of court.

The army began the process of court-martialing a soldier for aggravated assault because he had sex with two women without telling them he was infected with AIDS. One expert called it the first criminal prosecution for infecting another person with a disease through sexual intercourse.

THE MOST POIGNANT STORY OF THE YEAR

A fourth grade teacher at Harrison Grade School in Peoria, Illinois, asked her students to write an essay on how they'd use three wishes. One student's answer was that she "wished that her mother would stop beating her." The rest of the essay revealed a nightmare of child abuse. The teacher called police. The little girl and her four brothers and sisters were placed in foster care, and her parents were jailed.

IF THIS DOESN'T MAKE YOU WINCE...

Police in New York City caught up with what a local paper called a "one-man ear ring." A crack addict had allegedly conducted a reign of terror in the subway system. His crime—ripping gold earrings out of the earlobes of passengers.

HE NEVER SHOULD HAVE STOPPED FOR A BITE

In Raleigh, North Carolina, a Superior Court judge ordered murder suspect James E. Thomas to be drugged to sleep so molds could be made of his teeth. Thomas allegedly bit the breasts of his female victim before he strangled her, and the teeth marks were important evidence.

NOW STARRING IN "FLEECING THE TENANTS"

The New York State attorney general accused **Jay Weiss,** husband of actress **Kathleen Turner,** and three realtors of allegedly running a scheme to illegally sublet Manhattan apartments. Weiss and his partners agreed to repay $60,000 in overcharges to tenants and an additional $10,000 in legal fees.

CRIME AND PUNISHMENT

A liquor company executive who pleaded guilty to murder in a drunken driving case was released from jail after serving just one month of his twenty-year sentence. A circuit court judge released him because he thought one month was "punishment enough." There was no report on the reaction of the family of the sixty-one-year-old man who died.

CRIME FIGHTER'S WEAPON OF THE YEAR

Police Sergeant Robert Wolfgang of Albany, New York, explained how a local woman fought off a would-be purse snatcher: "She struck him repeatedly with a hot fudge sundae she was carrying. I know that sounds strange, but that's what happened."

NEXT TIME HE'LL REMEMBER HIS GLASSES

Sixty-one-year-old retired army sergeant Percy Washington of Rochester, New York, decided one day he wanted to kill his wife. He purchased a shotgun, then headed for church, intending to shoot her after Sunday services. The problem was, he had forgotten his glasses. Outside the church, he thought he spotted his wife behind the wheel of her car, so he leaned over the hood and shot her through the windshield. Unfortunately, the blind-as-a-bat ex-sergeant killed the wrong woman, a seventy-year-old parishoner who drove a similar-looking car.

NOW, THAT'S A CRIME

THE HIGH-TECH CRIME OF THE YEAR

A repairman in New York City was called to fix an automatic teller machine at a bank. While he made the repair, he attached a tape recorder to the device. The recorder taped all of the subsequent account numbers and identification codes punched into the machine by customers. The repairman proceeded to empty several accounts before he was caught.

To New Yorkers, the apartment sounded like a dream come true. The ad described it as a "small 1 bedroom, great neighborhood, exposed brick walls, $536 a month." One twenty-two year-old man saw the ad, inspected the place, then plunked down $1,214 for rent and security. Problem was, when he showed up to take possession, he found that over forty other people had paid the same deposit to the same woman. The con artist, who hadn't paid her rent for months, had fled, evidently looking for another apartment in some far-off spot.

HEY, I GOT A DUMB IDEA . . .

Two Bronx, New York, men broke into the reptile house at the Bronx Zoo and filched sixteen snakes, including four that were highly poisonous. The men apparently had no idea what to do with the snakes, which were still in their possession when they were apprehended a few days later.

THAT'S A LOT OF WHITE SHEETS

The nation's largest Ku Klux Klan group was ordered to pay $7 million in damages to Beulah Mae Donald, whose son was killed by two Klansmen. Among other things, Mrs. Donald was awarded the deed to the Klan's headquarters building—and maybe all the sheets inside.

THE SHARPEST CIVILIAN CRIME-FIGHTER AWARD...

Goes to the anonymous person in Seattle, Washington, whose hobby must be leafing through those grim "Wanted" posters hanging in post offices. Somehow, this person managed to connect a local physical therapist named Terrance Peter Jackson with a seventeen-year-old picture of a former leader of the radical Weather Underground who was wanted by the FBI for trying to blow up an ROTC office in 1970. After receiving the tip, the Feds arrested Jackson, who turned out to be **Silas Bissell,** who had once been listed as the "most wanted fugitive terrorist." We bet Bissell was more than a little surprised.

THE BEST NEW BUSINESS PLAN OF 1987

Henry Suchta and his daughter Shelby decided to open an antique store, hardly a new idea in the Auburn, New York, area. However, they found an ingenious way to stock the store: they looted private homes and the headquarters of the South Jefferson Historical Association of the Civil War. Unfortunately, they were nabbed by Auburn city police before they could reap the full benefits of their business plan.

SNOW BUNNY SLASHED

Ex-nun Kathleen Zanio was arrested by Milwaukee, Wisconsin, police for taking an ax and destroying a snow sculpture of a bikini-clad woman that sat on the lawn of a Milwaukee home. No word on whether the steamy statue was melting all the snowmen in the neighborhood.

THE 1987 BAD TASTE AWARD...

Goes to **Claus von Bulow,** who testified that he had credit cards issued to his live-in lover, **Andrea Reynolds,** in the name of his comatose wife, **Sunny.** Von Bulow said the cards were issued to buy things for **Cosima von Bulow,** Claus and Sunny's daughter. A Saks Fifth Avenue employee stated that Mrs. Reynolds used Sunny von Bulow's card to buy herself a pair of $390 slacks.

THE EMPLOYER OF THE YEAR AWARD

Might go to the **Du Pont Company.** In 1987, a Superior Court judge in Camden, New Jersey, awarded $1.4 million in damages to five Du Pont employees and the estate of a sixth because the company allegedly withheld medical records showing that the employees suffered from disease related to inhaling asbestos. The suit charged that Du Pont had failed to notify employees that required annual lung X-rays revealed spots on their lungs and that this failure had aggravated their illnesses and delayed treatment. One of the workers who filed the lawsuit died of lung cancer before the verdict was handed down.

THE 1987 POLICE-SCROOGE AWARD

We know cops have to enforce the law. But we think that police in St. Petersburg, Florida, might have been more than a little overzealous in tossing thirty-four-year-old Gary Sullivan into the slammer. His crime: stealing a couple of jars of baby food for his sick eight-month-old nephew. Sullivan, unemployed and broke, had been desperately trying to help support the little tyke.

NOW, THAT'S THE OLYMPIC SPIRIT

Former British Olympic medal winner **David Jenkins** and a University of Miami football coach were among thirty-four people indicted by the federal government for running a nationwide ring that controlled 70 percent of the black market in illegal steroids. The steroids, which are used by athletes and bodybuilders to beef up muscles, have been linked to liver cancer, heart disease, high blood pressure, and premature baldness. The indictment charged that the ring used strong-arm tactics and torture in running their multimillion-dollar-a-year racket.

WHY NOT A GENERAL?

The FBI arrested a Brooklyn, New York, man who had spent three years walking around the Fort Hamilton, New York, army base posing as a major. The Feds had absolutely no idea why the man carried on the charade.

THE LAWN ARM OF THE LAW

In Ishpeming, Michigan, one more crime has been added to existing misdeeds like rape, murder, and arson.

The crime: failure to mow the grass. The City Council passed a regulation making it illegal to let grass grow over twelve inches high.

CRIMINAL DICTION

The "criminal" could have been known as the Mumbler. A rather seedy-looking man, carrying no gun or robbery note, staggered into a branch of the First American Bank in Lansing, Michigan. He mumbled something to the frightened teller, who immediately forked over $1,300.

Soon, Lansing police officers and FBI agents were swarming all over the scene, putting out a dragnet that finally caught the culprit. He turned out to be a wino who'd staggered into the bank to mumble a request for fifty cents to buy a beer. The annoyed authorities couldn't file charges because drunken mumbling is not a crime.

What happened to the money? The happiest wino in the world drank up almost all of it before he was caught.

WE KNOW IT'S THE LAW, BUT . . .

Lake City, Michigan, police officer Patrick Bunce nailed fifty-three people for drunk driving in just eight months. His reward: the City Council fired him. It seems that the owners of the tourist town's five bars complained that Bunce was driving customers away, ruining their business. So the lawmakers did their duty, negotiating for Bunce's resignation. The officer finally gave in and quit when the so-called lawmakers offered him an immediate payment of $4,400 and weekly paychecks until he found another job.

WITNESSES YOU CAN TRUST

Two government witnesses in a White Plains, New York, Federal Court pleaded guilty to rifling the pocketbooks of jurors hearing the case.

THE LEAKIEST JAILS IN AMERICA

The Salem, Oregon, *Statesman-Journal* reported that the state prison system averaged more than two escapes daily.

DAD WAS A REAL HERO

Twenty-five-year-old Patrick Donahoe was riding in his car with his two-year-old son when he picked up a nineteen-year-old acquaintance. The rider pulled a knife and attacked father and son. The toddler was stabbed in the chest and slashed across the throat. The father was stabbed twenty times in the chest, back, arms, and legs; another wound penetrated his brain. After the attacker left them for dead, Donahoe wrote the attacker's name in the dirt, then starting crawling for help. Although his lungs partially collapsed, he managed to cover a mile in twelve agonizing hours. He finally reached an empty house, broke a window to get in, and called police. Both the father and son survived.

THE TRICYCLE GANG

After a desperate four-block chase, the police finally collared three desperadoes known as the Tricycle Gang. These hardened criminals had used a brick to blast their way into the Lily Ferguson Child Development Center in Waterloo, Iowa, and had then made off with three hot tricycles. The gang leader, age seven, was charged with juvenile delinquency. The cops let his two accomplices, age three and four, go free with a warning.

THE BEST LAID PLANS OF MICE AND MEN . . .

James Smithy of Wheaton, Illinois, thought he'd found the perfect way to beat check-forging charges. He forged his own death certificate, then celebrated when the authorities accepted it as genuine and had the charges dismissed.

Problem was, Smithy had for some reason listed drug and alcohol overdose as the cause of death. By sheer coincidence, the U.S. Census Bureau was doing a study on drug and alcohol deaths, and it sent a medical investigator to the hospital listed on the death certificate. Naturally, the hospital had never heard of Smithy. The cops soon traced him.

The subsequent investigation turned up another slight mistake that also might have exposed the phony death: Smithy supposedly died in July, but he renewed his driver's license in October.

THE U.S. CUSTOMS SERVICE AT WORK

Two U.S. Customs agents were more than a little interested when a Dominican businessman arrived in San Juan, Puerto Rico, with a bag containing $693,000 in cash and checks. According to charges filed in U.S. District Court, the two agents checked the man through customs, followed him from the airport, shot him to death, grabbed the money, then resigned from their jobs.

WE'VE HEARD OF BEING CASUAL, BUT . . .

In Fort Lauderdale, Florida, twenty-three-year-old Carl Watts was on trial for murder for having shot a friend in a dispute over $20. Watts proclaimed his innocence, but evidently grew bored with the proceedings—through most of the trial, he slept in his chair at the defense table.

Watts woke up just in time to hear the guilty verdict. The prosecutor said Watts's sleeping through the trial was "a great help."

MASQUERADE OF THE YEAR

Twenty-three-year-old Rodney Turner, wanted by the cops for two petty theft warrants, hid out for three months by posing as a student at a Milpitas, California, junior high school. Somehow Turner convinced the staff and students that he was fourteen years old. The charade fell apart when the school staff tried to find his parents. Turner served a short time in jail, but he got rave reviews as a student. Said the school psychologist, "I wish that a lot of other students here were as motivated as he was."

DRUG-TESTS LIAR

Dr. Delbert Lacefield, age fifty-three, of Oklahoma City, pleaded guilty to having faked the drug tests of railroad employees involved in three train accidents. Lacefield, supervisor of the Forensic Toxicology Research Unit of the Civil Aeromedical Institute of the Federal Aviation Administration, admitted having sent negative reports for recent drug use, even though he'd never tested the blood. In short, the doc lied.

VIOLENT OR VICTIMIZED?

Mary Beth Tinning of Schenectady, New York, was convicted of having murdered her three-year-old daughter Tami Lynne in December 1985. Police have also said they are suspicious of the deaths of seven of her eight other children who died in early childhood.

The defense attorney claimed Mrs. Tinning was a very unlucky woman who had been preyed upon by police. Witnesses, however, portrayed a woman who'd been largely indifferent to the death of her ninth child.

The other children who died, and their ages at death, were: Jennifer, seven days old; Joseph, Jr., two years; Barbara Ann, four years; Timothy, nineteen days; Nathan, five months; Mary Frances, three months; Jonathan, four months; and Michael, two years.

GOOD SAMARITANS GET A LOUSY REWARD

In Los Angeles, two teenagers chased down a twenty-eight-year-old man who had snatched the purse of a sixty-seven-year-old woman. The mugger, who was high on alcohol and cocaine at the time, died after he was apprehended. The L.A. district attorney's office charged the two teenagers with murder for having used excessive force in catching the man.

WALL STREET REACHES NEW HIGH

Nineteen employees, including sixteen stockbrokers, were arrested by federal authorities who charged they operated a widespread drug operation that traded cocaine for "inside information" as well as cash.

WANTED: 100-FOOT-TALL BURGLAR

Someone stole a 50-foot-high pair of blue jeans that normally adorned a balloon floating over Dunham's Athleisure sporting goods store in Amherst, New York. Police were on the lookout for any suspicious person about the size of the Jolly Green Giant.

STEALING LIKE DICKENS

It was a story reminiscent of Charles Dickens's novel, *Oliver Twist*, in which a character named Fagin controlled a gang of young pickpockets. Police in New York, New Jersey, and Connecticut were looking for a modern-day Fagin, a man known only as J.W., who controlled a gang of 150 young boys who were transported from New York City to suburban malls to shoplift. Each of the boys stole an average of $500 to $800 worth of designer clothes and sneakers per day.

IN THE STUPID CRIMES DEPARTMENT

An IRS mail clerk was arrested by the FBI for stealing tax returns at a processing center that receives returns from three states. Does this guy have a W-2 fetish?

AMONG THE CRIMES THAT MAKE SENSE

A postal clerk in Baton Rouge, Louisiana, pleaded guilty to having stolen some of the cash-laden mail addressed to television evangelist **Jimmy Swaggart.**

FAKED ART THEFT

A Texas oil heir, forty-five-year-old **William O'Boyle,** was arrested in New York and charged with having faked the theft of $1.8 million in pre-Columbian art works in order to defraud an insurance company. According to the Manhattan D.A., the works were never worth more than $200,000.

O'Boyle's secretary, **Patricia Roberts,** returned the art works to the insurance company six months after the theft. Six months after that, Roberts and her husband were ambushed by a gunman outside their home. The husband was killed and Patricia was in a coma for five months before recovering. The shootings remain unsolved.

DECISIONS, DECISIONS, DECISIONS

Twenty-nine-year-old bank manager David Messer had a decision to make, and he decided to write down the pros and cons. The subject of his dilemma was whether or not to run off with $161,000 in cash from the bank.

The pros Messer listed were: "You won't get another chance again. Won't flip out with wife and kid; travel anywhere, live on islands, meet many women, party and prevent heart attacks, life stimulation, believe that it's inevitable and . . . the last time, can't get transfer, drugs, credit background and lie detector for honesty."

The cons, in Messer's words: "Loss of loved ones, regret with no return possible, money won't last forever, can't get other I.D., if caught will go to jail."

What would you decide? Messer's final statement was: "Dave, let's face the hard facts. You are a loser." So he opted to split with the money, leaving the note behind. Along with $161,000 in cash from the vault and automatic teller machines he took 389 American Express travelers checks, 300 American Express money orders, and 102 U.S. government savings bonds.

A MODEL OF CONSISTENCY

Railroad worker Michael T. March, age thirty-nine, of Nashville, Tennessee, was a model of consistency on the job for ten years. He was not, however, the kind of model the company wanted its other workers to emulate. March was fired for having stolen something from his employers on every single workday over that ten-year period. Equipment worth $178,000 was recovered from his house, and he was ordered to pay another $14,239 in damages.

IF AT FIRST YOU DON'T SUCCEED ...

A Miami, Florida, man was arrested after a $175,000 helicopter he was trying to steal crashed moments after takeoff. It turned out the man was already on probation —for trying to steal another helicopter. Oh, by the way—the man had absolutely no pilot training.

EASTER SCROOGE

Just a few days before Easter, Brian Allen was promoting the holiday spirit by peddling some hand-painted Easter eggs on the streets of Manhattan. Before he could say Peter Rabbit, the cops picked him up and hauled him off to jail for illegal vending. He spent twenty-four hours in the slammer before a judge ruled that selling Easter eggs isn't a crime.

Oh, yes, a side note to the story: Maybe the cops were reacting to Allen's "street" name—he's known as Brain Damage.

AN EXPLOSIVE TRIAL

Accused LSD dealer Robert Gary was about to face his fifth charge for peddling hallucinogenic drugs, and it appears that he didn't relish the idea of a jail sentence. So he made himself a bomb, carried it into the Kokomo, Indiana, courthouse, and set it off. Gray killed himself and injured ten others, including his lawyer.

A MAN'S GOT A RIGHT TO HIS OPINION

The U.S. Supreme Court ruled unconstitutional the firing of a Harris County, Texas, deputy constable who had said of the attempt on Ronald Reagan's life, "If they go for him again, I hope they get him." Commented the assistant county attorney, "I think I'll throw up."

DECEPTION OF THE YEAR

Since 1978, Robert Blackmon, who'd been sentenced for the murder of his wife, had rolled around the prison in a wheelchair. Blackmon had been wounded in Vietnam, and the entire prison staff of Avon Park Correctional Institution in Fort Myers, Florida, believed he was a paraplegic—until he shocked authorities by jumping out the wheelchair, seizing a guard, taking the officer's gun, and escaping with hostages.

NOW, THAT'S A CRIME

Six people in Miami, Florida, were indicted in connection with the distribution of one million fake birth control pills. You talk about surprised crime victims . . .

TALES OF THE MEDICAL PROFESSION

A man in Queens, New York, who described himself as a plastic surgeon although he had no formal training, allegedly botched breast augmentation surgery on a patient. Then he panicked, keeping the bleeding woman in his office for forty-two hours—over one and a half days—without seeking emergency help.

Two years ago a Miami prostitute, Wendy Ann Blankenship, learned she was carrying the AIDS virus, but she continued to sleep with hundreds of men without telling them. She'd been arrested for prostitution fifteen times over those two years. Blankenship told a reporter, "You just can't tell everybody you go into a car with that you have it—they'll kill you. I usually carry condoms, but most of my clients don't want to use them.

I tell them I'm clean—they won't date me if I'm not clean."

SIGNS OF THE TIMES

New York City's Metropolitan Transportation Authority announced a ban on "take-one" ads—that is, adds to which coupons were attached so that subway riders could take one home. The reason for the ban: Vandals were allegedly removing the staples that held the pads together and using them to scratch the windows of subway cars.

INNOCENT AND GUILTY

The good news for Teddy Dixon of Chuckey, Tennessee, was that the jury returned a verdict of not guilty on arson charges. The bad news was that the judge held him in contempt of court for failing to show up to hear the verdict. Dixon got ten days in the slammer.

KNUCKLED UNDER

A man was indicted in Manhattan for beating to death a four-month-old girl. The key evidence: An impression of the man's knuckles exactly matched indentations in the child's body.

ORDERED TO COMMIT A CRIME

Travis Loofbourrow of Houston, Texas, was finally caught after he had stolen $340,000 from twelve automatic teller machines. Bank officials were so baffled by how he did it that a deal was worked with the court: Loofbourrow would break into a thirteenth machine while bank officials videotaped his "crime."

BIRDNAPPER BECOMES JAILBIRD

In Lakeport, California, a judge ordered that Richard Garner be "caged" for three years for birdnapping a macaw, then holding the bird for a $1,500 ransom.

WAS THAT CONSIDERED A STRIP SEARCH?

A thirty-one-year-old man robbed the patrons at a New Rochelle, New York, nightclub, then ordered them to strip so they wouldn't follow him. As the patrons were disrobing, the cops showed up. The robber then took off his own clothes and tried to mingle with the patrons. But the victims recognized him even in the buff, and the guy was tried and sentenced to ten to twenty years in the slammer.

CALL-GIRL BILLS

A twenty-five-year-old Los Angeles man, Jonathan Margolis, was charged with having stolen $37,000 from his employer to pay his phone bill. Why was the bill so large? Margolis evidently spent an average of ninety minutes a day, 365 days a year, calling telephone sex numbers.

THE CRIMINAL WAS GIFT-WRAPPED

The residents of a Los Angeles apartment complex evidently got fed up with car thefts. They caught a man stealing a car stereo, then called police. When the cops arrived, they found the suspect trussed up tightly, gagged, and sitting in the middle of the lawn.

DOUBLE TROUBLE

Talk about a bad day. Darryl Birge, age thirty-one, was in court facing a $900 robbery charge. As he was escorted out of the courtroom, he was spotted by a twenty-five-year-old woman being tried on a forgery charge. The woman started screaming for police, and after she told her story, Birge was marched back into the courtroom and charged with having raped the woman.

Birge had previously served eight years in prison for rape.

EVERYONE NEEDS A HOBBY

You would think that four days after he won the U.S. Boxing Association cruiserweight championship, Sherman Griffin would still have been celebrating. Instead, he allegedly went to a Houston motel and tried to rob a couple, beating down the door to their room with his fists. However, the champ was felled by shots fired by a motel clerk. Now he's waiting for the judge's decision.

MOVIE FANS SUSPENDED

Where were the police officers in San Jose, California, when citizens needed them? One day five of the cops —all of them on duty—were in a movie theater watching *Beverly Hills Cop II*. Somehow, the police chief didn't think that was very funny—he gave them a few unpaid days off. Wonder if the cops took advantage by seeing a few more movies?

HIS ROLE WAS PRISON ESCAPEE

Daniel F. Duane, a shrewd inmate serving a fifteen-year sentence at Stateville Correctional Institute in Joliet, Illinois, got the role of his life while a movie was being filmed in the prison. After the day's shooting for a film entitled *Weeds*, starring Nick Nolte, Duane convinced a member of the movie crew that he was a prison guard. He talked the guy into giving him a ride on the equipment truck, then waved at guards as they drove out the gates. Once outside the walls, Duane headed for the hills—without waiting for applause.

LOYAL OR DUMB?

When his brother was arrested on robbery and kidnapping charges, Carmine Fudge of East Chatham, New York, put up his entire nest egg, including his 100-acre farm, to post a $100,000 bond for his brother. George Fudge, the brother, promptly took off, resulting in the forfeit of the bond and the loss of the farm. But even though George had taken off, Carmine testified on his brother's behalf when George was tried "in absentia." The conclusion: George was convicted, but he was still on the lam. Carmine, who lost everything, said, "Blood is thicker than water." No word on whether the word "thick" applied to George's skull.

DEADLY COMPUTER GAME

According to police, Wyley Gates, seventeen, and his friend, Damian Rossney, sixteen, stole two computers from their high school in Hudson, New York. For the next six weeks, they used the computers to program a deadly game they called Infierno, the Spanish word for hell. When the computer fantasy was finished, charged police, Gates calmly turned it into reality by killing his father, his brother, his cousin, and his father's girlfriend with a .38 caliber revolver.

BLOOD FOR DRUGS RING

Twenty-one people, including two doctors, were arrested in Detroit for running a "blood for drugs" ring that cheated Blue Cross and Medicaid out of at least $10 million. In the scam, drug addicts were given narcotics without prescriptions in exchange for blood samples that were sent for testing and falsely billed to insurers.

A REALLY HOT LINE

Some pimp in New York City came up with one of the most imaginative recruiting schemes of the year. The pimp called a hot line that took calls from runaway kids. He told hot line officials that the number of a shelter for runaways had been changed. The new number the pimp gave the hot line wasn't the shelter, but a phone booth in Manhattan's Port Authority Bus Terminal. The phony number was in operation for three weeks before hot line officials discovered the deception. The pimp escaped, after luring an undetermined number of kids into prostitution.

TALK ABOUT SLIPPERY CHARACTERS...

Police in Hammond, Indiana, had a real bizarre case on their hands when twenty-three-year-old Darnell Mardis allegedly set his own house on fire. When fire fighters doused the blaze, police rushed in. They found Mardis sitting in his own bathtub—completely covered with butter from head to toe. Officers had a lot of trouble hauling in the very slippery man, who was charged with arson, assaulting a police officer, and resisting arrest.

In 1980, John Buettner-Janusch, a professor of anthropology at New York University, was convicted of using students to manufacture Quaaludes, LSD, and synthetic cocaine in his lab. Evidently, he resented the judge's sentence of five years in jail. On the eve of Valentine's Day, an anonymous gift of candy arrived at the judge's home. His wife sampled four of the goodies—then was rushed to the hospital to have her stomach pumped. Buettner-Janusch was arrested again, charged this time with poisoning the candy.

SHERIFF USES FLOWER POWER

Augusta, Maine, sheriff Frank Hackett has proved to be one of the nation's most clever lawmen in tracking down citizens who failed to pay fines or appear in court. In 1986, Hackett sent delinquents an invitation from USA Cable Television Network to come to a hotel to audition for a film. USA, in this case, stood for "U Should've Appeared," and the six people who responded were arrested.

This year, Hackett did even better. He put signs on a van advertising the FTA (for "Failure to Appear") flower delivery service, then loaded the van with flowers and balloons. Eleven of the twenty-five people Hackett was after fell for the ruse, opened the doors of their homes, and were hauled in by deputies.

LAWYER JAILED FOR REFUSING TO LIE

Miami, Florida, attorney Ellis Rubin discovered that a murder suspect he was defending planned to lie under oath during his trial. He tried to withdraw from the case, but a judge ordered to him to continue. When Rubin refused, the judge ordered him jailed for twenty-nine days for refusing to commit what he called "court-ordered perjury."

SOCK IT TO SUZUKI

A jury in Los Angeles ruled that Suzuki, the Japanese motorcycle company, had deliberately stolen a design for shock absorbers invented by a California teenager. The court awarded the inventor $19 million in royalties.

WARNING! BEAUTY CONTESTS CAN BE HAZARDOUS TO YOUR HEALTH

Joshua Wagshell of Brooklyn, New York, spotted posters on the subway soliciting entries in the Miss Ronrico Rum contest. He decided to submit a photograph of a beautiful woman—who didn't happen to be his wife.

Shortly afterward, his wife found the photograph. Allegedly, she selected a .357 magnum from her husband's arsenal of weapons and shot him in the chest.

Thirteen associates of political extremist **Lyndon LaRouche** were arrested on charges that they had fraudulently solicited $30 million in loans that they had no intention of repaying. According to authorities, LaRouche followers would talk to people, especially the elderly in airports, urging them to buy publications. Later, they'd contact the people repeatedly by phone, requesting large "loans" and offering high interest rates in return. Of the $30 million they "borrowed," however, only $250,000 was repaid.

3.
AMONG THE THINGS YOU DIDN'T WANT TO KNOW...

ALL OF US KNOW a few people who refuse to read the newspapers or watch the news because they'd just rather not know about all the depressing things that are happening in our world. The rest of us can appreciate that sentiment (is our life better for knowing that AIDS exists?), but most of us go right ahead and get our somewhat masochistic pleasure from hearing about what life could have in store for us.

One such story came out of Florida last year. It seems that the 1987 Florida State Legislature made a whopper of a mistake when it innocently set out to establish a statewide procedure for obtaining permits to carry concealed weapons. By passing that law, however, the legislators inadvertently wiped out all local gun control laws, leaving citizens free to carry weapons openly in public. Said the state attorney general in a letter to the governor, "The possibility of openly armed gangs hanging around street corners, bikers traveling down a city street or major highway with shotguns or rifles cradled in their arms, and gunmen parading through shopping malls, I find to be terrifying." So, no doubt, did Florida citizens, who joined in a request to call the legislature back into special session to right the wrong.

Another story no one really wanted to watch aired on a West German television show called *Monitor*, which is kind of a German *60 Minutes*. A July 28, 1987, broadcast included a health segment featuring revolting pictures, in close-up, of live roundworms being pulled from "pan-ready" fish fillets. The program went on to explain that the thin worms, which are less than an inch long, can settle in the intestines, causing painful obstructions and even tumors.

The program neglected to tell viewers that serious illnesses from fish parasites are rare. So some viewers panicked, and the German fish industry found itself fighting for its life. In one city alone, two hundred wholesalers canceled orders for fish. Industry observers predicted it would be months before the industry recovered.

In this chapter, you'll find a lot of other things you didn't want to know. But we suspect that won't keep you from reading on.

꼭

The Federal Centers for Disease Control reported that as many as 95 percent of this country's 10,000 severe hemophiliacs have been infected with AIDS. The problem developed because a severe hemophiliac is exposed to the blood of 800,000 to 1 million people each year, and most became infected before hospitals began heat-treating all blood to prevent AIDS transmission. An estimated 30 to 50 percent of people with moderate to mild hemophilia have also been infected.

꼭

A poll by Crane's Chicago Business revealed that 20 percent of U.S. business executives have offered a bribe to a government inspector.

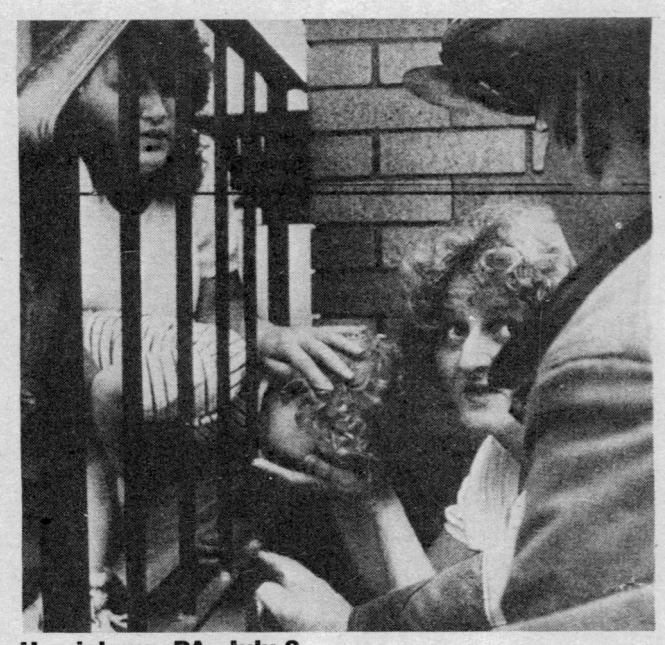

Harrisburg, PA, July 8

Harrisburg firefighter Rob Sullivan removed Carlos Rivera's head from the Riveras' porch railing with a device known as "Jaws of Life." Neither his mother, Meta Maldonado (left) nor his babysitter, Jody Carson, knew how the 18-month-old child got stuck. (Stuart Leask)

THE MOST UNBELIEVABLE STORY OF 1987

Representatives of the United Nicaraguan Opposition Front, the umbrella group for all the Contra factions, told U.S. Senate investigators that they'd never bothered to ask where all the money deposited in their bank account came from.

AFTER THE KILLER BEES COMES . . .

The Asian tiger mosquito, an especially fierce biter that may carry dengue fever and La Crosse encephalitis. These mosquitoes apparently entered the United States in used tires that arrived in Houston a couple of years ago and, as of the summer of 1987, had spread to thirteen eastern states.

MORE GOOD NEWS FOR LOVERS

It's turning out these days that the only safe place for lovers is under a cold shower. Dr. Nester C. del Rosario, in an article in the *New England Journal of Medicine*, reported that hickeys received while necking can give you herpes. Next thing you know, we'll find out shaking hands causes cancer.

NEWS OF ROYALTY YOU DIDN'T WANT TO HEAR...

A new book by Timothy Benford revealed that early in their marriage, **Prince Philip** entered **Queen Elizabeth's** bedroom "wearing plastic vampire teeth. He said he wasn't a prince but a count—Count Dracula—and started chasing her around." Boy, we're glad we know that.

THE UGLY DUCKLING WAS REALLY A SWAN?

Recent research reveals that fairy tale author **Hans Christian Andersen** apparently lied about his life history. Andersen wrote that he was born in abject poverty, was so ugly as a child that he had no friends, but later became wealthy and famous. The truth: Andersen was the illegitimate son of a prince who later became King Christian VIII of Denmark.

AMERICA'S BIGGEST EGOS

M magazine compiled a list of the ten famous Americans who, as the magazine gently put it, had the most "boundless self-esteem." The list:

THINGS YOU DIDN'T WANT TO KNOW...

Oral Roberts
Dan Rather
New York Governor **Mario Cuomo**
Playwright-director **Robert Wilson**
Bill Cosby
George Steinbrenner
Lee Iacocca
Henry Kissinger
New York real estate mogul **Donald Trump**
Shirley MacLaine

AS IF YOU DIDN'T HAVE ENOUGH TO WORRY ABOUT...

Astronomers discovered that massive, energy-sucking "black holes" are the centers of two of our neighboring galaxies. According to the scientists, these mysterious holes could eventually gobble up the entire systems. Though there's no proof that our own Milky Way could have a hungry black hole, too, we wouldn't advise making any plans beyond the next million years or so.

AMONG THE THINGS YOU DIDN'T WANT TO KNOW ABOUT ENGLISH HISTORY...

Archaeologists have discovered that Stone Age Britons practiced cannibalism.

HORSES HAVING TROUBLE IN THE SADDLE

We humans aren't the only ones whose sex lives are suffering today. Research presented at the annual meeting of the American Veterinary Medical Association revealed that up to one-fourth of all stallions are having sexual problems, primarily because of stress and drug use. No word on whether Dr. Ruth is going to be the keynote speaker at next year's meeting.

When the cost of a postage stamp rises to a quarter, as approved by the Postal Commission, you'll be able to make a one-minute phone call anywhere in the United States for less than it will cost to mail a letter.

IF IT COSTS $2.1 MILLION, WE'LL LET YOU DIE

Government agencies have put a value of about $2 million on a human life, when balancing the expense of banning suspected cancer-causing substances against the benefits of lower cancer-death rates.

THE JOYS OF PIGGING OUT

Seventh grader Ezra Wise of Clearwater, Florida, conducted a science project designed to see how effective a health-food diet really was. He bought two rats, Tom and Jerry. Jerry ate a healthful diet; Tom pigged out on brownies, ice cream, and pizza. The results: Jerry the Rat soon croaked on the health-food diet; Tom the Rat was thriving after five months on junk food.

SLEAZY CELEBRITY NEWS...

Barbara Seaman, in her biography of the late famous author **Jacqueline Susann**, claimed that Jackie had a big crush on **Ethel Merman**. Susann allegedly got Merman drunk one night, then started smootching with her in public.

BULLETIN: WEST PALM BEACH A SUBURB OF LAGOS, NIGERIA

Geologists announced the discovery that Florida was a part of Africa that drifted away about 200 million years ago.

THE BARE FACTS

Helena Shultz, wife of Secretary of State **George Shultz**, confirmed that her husband did indeed have a Princeton tiger tattooed on his buttocks. She said, "When the children were young, they used to run up and touch it, and he would growl and they would run away."

THE WORST FINANCIAL ADVICE OF THE YEAR

A brokerage firm announced a study that linked the rise and fall of the stock market to costumes worn by **Vanna White** on *Wheel of Fortune*. Said a financial analyst, "If she sports a white strapless dress, a 'buy' program appears to follow. 'Sell' programs are initiated if she wears high-necked garments."

THE NEW PRODUCT YOU WANTED TO KNOW ABOUT LEAST

A new company, New Williamsburg, Inc., was formed to manufacture and sell caskets that look exactly like regular furniture. For example, one model resembles a piece of Art Deco furniture; another looks like a Danish teak coffee table. Just the thing if you're entertaining at the mausoleum.

HONESTY IN PSYCHIATRY

A nationwide poll reported in the *American Journal of Orthopsychiatry* revealed that two-thirds of psychiatrists have treated patients who've been sexually involved with other therapists, contacts which they believe were harmful and for which therapists can lose their licenses. But these same public-spirited individuals reported the abusive conduct of their colleagues in only 8 percent of cases.

YOUR TAX DOLLARS AT WORK

Senator **Quentin Burdick** of North Dakota obtained an appropriation of $8 million for North Dakota State University for the study of weeds. Another senator questioned why, "after millions of years of history with weeds, all of a sudden it's critically important to finance a weed center."

THIS DOESN'T ADD UP

Emergency Medicine magazine suggested that patients who have trouble producing urine samples for medical tests solve their problem by reciting multiplication tables. Huh?

About $40 million is raised annually by 381,980 charity-sponsored gum-ball and candy machines—the ones you see everywhere. Problem is, according to the Orlando, Florida, *Sentinel*, only 13 percent of all that money actually goes to charity.

MORE SLEAZY GOSSIP

The hostess of a $50,000-a-ticket charity banquet held in Palm Beach, Florida, to honor **Princess Diana** and **Prince Charles** was a former nude model and columnist for a raunchy British soft-core porn magazine. **Pat Kluge**, the thirty-six-year-old wife of seventy-one-year-old billionaire **John Kluge**, was once married to the publisher of the English sex magazine, *Knave*. In addition to posing nude for full frontal pictures, Pat wrote a column detailing the bedroom quirks of men of various nationalities.

No word on whether Pat and Diana exchanged confidences at the banquet.

THINGS YOU DIDN'T WANT TO KNOW... 91

The Federal Centers for Disease Control announced that up to half of all homeless people in the United States may be infected with tuberculosis.

According to *Newsweek* magazine, between 20 and 40 percent of the 57,000 Catholic priests in the United States are gay, and half of those are practicing homosexuals. Another 20 percent of Catholic priests are sexually active heterosexuals.

THE WORST NEW FOOD PRODUCT

What's in that "seafood salad" that looks so much like crab? It's imitation seafood known as surimi, "a surimi-based crab analogue." Surimi comes from pollack, a cheap whitefish that's washed and minced to produce a block of stuff that's tasteless, colorless, and odorless. This appetizing stuff is then dyed and flavored with chemical additives to supposedly taste like crab, shrimp, lobster, or other more expensive "non-analogue" products. Sales of the fake fish have jumped 1400 percent in the last five years.

IN THE DEPRESSING NEWS DEPARTMENT...

A survey of 30,000 El Paso, Texas, schoolchildren showed that one-fifth of them, a total of 6,000 kids, admitted to sniffing spray paint or glue. A full 40 percent regularly used drugs or alcohol.

THE 1987 SPORT OF THE YEAR

Looking for novel thrills and chills? At the Hamilton Country Fair in Ohio you can enjoy a new sport: pig racing. Spurred on by dangling Oreo cookies, the fastest porkers in the Midwest scoot down a 180-foot track at speeds up to 20 mph. One question: Does the winner bring home the bacon?

IN THE HOPELESS-CAUSES DEPARTMENT...

The city of Peoria, Illinois, paid a St. Louis, Missouri, public relations firm $60,000 to try to change the image of Peoria, which is generally thought of as a boring, dumpy town. Good luck.

TALES OF THE BOOB TUBE

A speech therapist speaking at a national convention charged that TV cult figure **Max Headroom**, with his fractured speech, was encouraging children to stutter. A publicist for ABC-TV disagreed, saying Headroom's speech was "a computer glitch, not a stutter."

RONALD McDONALD SAVES THE EARTH

McDonald's announced that it would stop serving Big Macs and other sandwiches in foam containers made with chlorofluorocarbons, chemicals that may be destroying the earth's ozone layer. Noble, but why were they using the stuff in the first place?

COLONEL NORTH CLONE

Inspired by the story of Lieutenant Colonel **Oliver North**, Abel Beets of Jackson, Michigan, decided to start his own business. For $9,000 he bought a five-horsepower paper shredder. He put the shredder in the back of his van and established his venture, called Data Destruction. Beets drives around destroying papers for a price. He bragged that he could shred the contents of a three-drawer file cabinet in twelve minutes. Ollie, what's your best time?

FUNNIEST CELEBRITY PARTY OF THE YEAR

Joan Collins threw a "Get Rid of Peter Party" in celebration of her pending divorce from **Peter Holm**. The bash was attended by more than a hundred celebrity guests, some of whom wore T-shirts with mottoes like: Holm Sweet Holm, Holm Wrecker, A House Is Not a Holm, and Holm Savings & Loan.

YOUNG ENTREPRENEUR OF THE YEAR

Sixteen-year-old Robert Encarnacao, a high school junior in Amherst, Massachusetts, asked the Amherst Regional School Committee for permission to buy and install vending machines to dispense condoms in the bathrooms of all junior and senior high schools. Needless to say, the committee's going to check out the opinion of parents before giving this enterprising young man the go-ahead.

FEAR OF FLYING

Eastern Airlines suspended its practice of giving a free drink to passengers whose flights had been delayed more than an hour. The reason: The airline had so many delays that the monthly tab for the free booze reached a whopping $144,000.

LIGHTNING STRIKES

The private Lightning Protection Institute says government figures on the number of people killed annually by lightning are all wrong. Although the Weather Service said sixty-eight people were killed last year, the LPI said the true figure could be as high as four hundred. Among places struck by lightning: a National Weather Service office.

DULLEST NEWS OF THE YEAR

Psychologist Mark Leary of Wake Forest University in Winston-Salem, North Carolina, is doing a study on why boring people are boring. Our question: How does he find people who admit they're boring? The answer's probably too boring to bother with.

MODERN SALES PROMOTION

Some sort of first for newspaper sales promotion was recorded when the Boston *Phoenix* tucked a condom into each of the 128,000 copies it distributed one week.

CREDIT CARDS CAN PINCH MORE THAN YOUR BUDGET

The *Harvard Medical School Letter* reported a new health hazard for men: Stuffing a wallet with too many credit cards and then carrying the wallet in your back pocket can pinch your sciatic nerve and lead to severe leg pain.

IF YOU THINK THE SUBWAYS ARE DANGEROUS

A study of highway accident statistics revealed that people who live in the rural West are one hundred times more likely to be killed in an auto accident than people who live in big cities.

SO MUCH FOR THE PRIDE BEING BACK

A grand jury indicted **Chrysler Motors** and two managers of its assembly plants on charges of having sold more than 60,000 cars that had previously been driven by company managers. According to the Justice Department, some of the cars had been involved in accidents, then cosmetically fixed without informing dealers or customers. The investigation into the tampering came about when Missouri state highway patrolmen reported that they had stopped Chrysler executives for speeding —and the executives had said they didn't know how fast they were going because their odometers were disconnected.

MORE REASSURANCE FOR AIRLINE PASSENGERS

When the FAA tested security at twenty-eight major airports, they discovered that more than 20 percent of concealed weapons made it past the security checkpoint.

YOU ARE WHAT YOU EAT

Diagionstic Industries of California is marketing a salmonella-poisoning test kit, with which you can check food before you dine. The cost of equipment to test three dishes: $5. If you eat in places where you're likely to need the kit, that's more than the cost of dinner.

ANOTHER HOSPITAL HORROR STORY

A Florida judge told Palm Beach Gardens Medical Center to stop stiffing patients by jacking up prices on equipment as much as 2,000 percent. An example: the hospital charged $15.50 for a disposable razor worth $1.37. Ouch!

MORE GOOD NEWS ABOUT PSYCHOTHERAPY

Psychiatrists recommended that **John W. Hinckley, Jr.,** who was confined to a mental hospital after shooting President **Ronald Reagan** in an attempt to impress **Jodie Foster**, be given a pass to leave the hospital to spend time with his parents—even though evidence was uncovered that Hinckley had passed his time in prison by exchanging letters with convicted mass murderers.

YOUR SPOUSE COULD BE HAZARDOUS TO YOUR HEALTH

According to a study by a professor at Louisiana State

University, a nonsmoker who marries a smoker doubles the risk of developing lung cancer.

THE GREAT CLOCK CRISIS

When exactly is 12:00 P.M.? According to a New Jersey appeals court, no one knows. The court made that statement in throwing out a $10 parking fine against a Wildwood, New Jersey, man, who claimed a ban on parking until 12:00 P.M. meant noon, not midnight.

A researcher at the University of Rochester School of Medicine reported that water beds give people heartburn by twisting the body and causing stomach acid to back up into the esophagus.

The National Charities Information Bureau discovered that the United Cancer Council, Inc., which raised $7 million to fight cancer, spent over 93 percent of that money on fund-raising. Even that percentage was better than the previous year, in which just $15,000 of the council's $5.1 million budget went to fighting cancer, while 97 percent went to fund-raising.

A Conrail engineer whose locomotive ran through a stop sign and collided with an Amtrak train, killing sixteen people, had a driving record marred with numerous serious violations. Commented Ross Capon of the Association of Railroad Passengers, "The obvious question is why the hell he was allowed to drive a train when he can't even drive a car."

FILM BLOOPERS

Jack Weyland, a physics professor at South Dakota School of Mines and Technology, entertained the American Physics Society and the American Association of Physics Teachers with scenes from Hollywood films that defied the laws of physics. Some examples:

- Remember Superman catching Lois Lane as she fell from the top of a building? According to Weyland, in real life Lois would have been traveling so fast that she would have hit Superman's arms with a sickening splat.
- *Star Wars* follies: Because there's no air in space to diffuse light and carry sound waves,
    - —you couldn't see laser beams from the side;
    - —you couldn't hear the sound of space fighters exploding;
    - —space ships couldn't bank as they turn, like fighters in Earth's atmosphere.

- King Kong's body would collapse into a heap, because a gorilla's bone structure couldn't support his weight at that size.
- Indiana Jones would have needed a crane to run off with the huge golden head that he somehow manages to carry in one hand in *Raiders of the Lost Ark*.

MORE NEWS OF THE NATIONAL SECURITY COUNCIL

When **Oliver North** got his important job at the National Security Council, his security check was evidently so sloppy that it failed to discover that North had spent three weeks in Bethesda Naval Hospital for treatment of emotional problems six years before he joined the President's staff. Several pages dealing with that hospitalization had been removed from the "outpatient treatment record" that every member of the military is supposed to carry.

SLEEPING PILLS FOR PLANTS?

Another entry in the Worst New Products Department is a substance developed by Weyerhaeuser. Injected into plants, it puts them into a kind of permanent "sleep." In this state, they look and feel like real plants, but they don't grow and don't need light or water. Just what the world needs, real fake plants.

GOVERNMENT BY LOOTING

Time magazine reported that more than one hundred politicians have faced criminal investigations involving alleged misdoings while in office. Our favorite in 1987:

C. McClain Haddow, former chief of staff at the Department of Health and Human Services, was indicted for fraudulently obtaining $33,540 from the T. Bear Foundation, which he helped create to encourage children to wash their hands.

Looks like America needs a foundation to keep political appointees clean.

A new study showed that chocolate, a longtime lovers' cure for heartache, is a major cause of heartburn.

MRS. O'LEARY'S COW CLEARED OF ARSON

All you bovine lovers can rest easy—Mrs. O'Leary's cow has been judged innocent of having started the Great Chicago Fire that destroyed 17,000 buildings in 1871. An arson investigator for the Federal Bureau of Alcohol, Tobacco and Firearms examined the evidence, then proclaimed it was Mrs. O'Leary herself who accidentally touched a lamp to tinder-dry hay.

Senator **William Proxmire** of Wisconsin announced that the Pentagon had spent $59,000 over the last six years for playing cards embossed with the vice-presidential seal, which were given away to passengers on Vice President **George Bush's** plane.

TAX NEWS YOU DIDN'T WANT TO HEAR

Burlington, Vermont, residents are complaining about the town's "view tax"—an extra 5 to 10 percent added to the property tax of homes that have a good view of the rolling green hills surrounding the town. The town also adds an extra 15 percent to the assessment of homes classified as "contemporary."

KILLER TRUCKS

The number of accidents involving trucks soared from 32,000 in 1983 to over 40,000 in 1987. Random inspections of trucks on the highway showed that 30 to 40 percent were operating with serious mechanical problems.

IN CASE YOU WERE PLANNING A TRIP TO ALASKA BY MOTORCYCLE...

The Anchorage, Alaska, Supreme Court ruled that members of the Hell's Angels motorcycle gang should be allowed to wear their gang jackets in the Crazy Horse, a bar that featured nude dancers. Sounds like one of the great constitutional issues of our times.

HONEY, PASS THE TOFU

A federal meat inspector testified in Congress that in American meat plants, "the flies have been getting

THINGS YOU DIDN'T WANT TO KNOW... 105

meaner, the roaches fatter, and the rats bolder." He went on to say that the label on meat products should be changed from "USDA Inspected and Approved" to "Eat at Your Own Risk." Testimony was taken after the National Academy of Sciences reported that Americans suffered from several million cases of food poisoning annually because federal inspectors failed to detect contamination at poultry processing plants.

DISSOLVO

Gilbreth International, Inc., of Bensalem, Pennsylvania, developed a new product called Dissolvo. What is it? It's a substance that looks and feels like regular paper but dissolves almost instantly in water. The company was a bit embarrassed, however, when police in a Chicago suburb learned that organized crime had discovered Dissolvo—the mob was using it to record gambling information, which could be destroyed with one bucket of water.

CHECK YOUR CHECKS

The federal government wants a new law requiring that government checks be cashed within six months or be declared worthless. The reason: The Treasury has trouble keeping track of an estimated 5.5 million checks worth $1.2 billion that are at least a year old.

Last year the government paid $32,221.40 to 361 people who cashed checks that were over thirty years old. The oldest check, dated April 19, 1919, was written to a Nebraska woman who had waited a cautious sixty-seven years before collecting $1.01 interest on a bond. The largest old check cashed was for $8,606 and was made out to a Michigan man as a 1954 tax refund.

GREED, JUNIOR STYLE

The greed in American society has spread to high school students, according to a poll taken by General Dynamics. Some 75 percent of high school students want to be president of a corporation, but only one in five would consider being President of the United States —a job that pays a measly $200,000 a year.

IN CASE YOU DIDN'T HAVE ENOUGH TO WORRY ABOUT...

A New York State scientific panel reported a study showing that children who lived near power lines were twice as prone to leukemia and brain cancer as children who lived far away from power lines. All you have to do, then, is move to a tent in the middle of the Arctic Circle.

A DECISION BRITISH MEN DIDN'T WANT TO HEAR

Declaring that swimsuits are "outmoded," officials declared that contestants in the Miss Great Britain contest will no longer parade in swimwear.

SIGNS OF THE TIMES

The 210 graduates of the Harvard University Public Health School celebrated the end of their schooling in a novel way—by tossing condoms inscribed in Latin to spectators. The condoms, packaged in white envelopes warning against AIDS, read: "Harvard School of Public Health Class of 1987" and "*Ad Venerem Securiorem*," which means "safe sex" in Latin.

CONDOM SCANDAL

The U.S. Food and Drug Administration announced that more than one out of every five batches of condoms it tested failed a water-leakage test.

MAYBE IT'S TIME TO CHECK YOUR DOCTOR'S PUPILS

A researcher reported that one in five American doctors, as many as 60,000 physicians, abuses drugs or alcohol. Almost 40 percent of these abusers are injecting drugs with needles.

OH, NO, HERE WE GO AGAIN

South Carolina legislator **Woody Aydlette**, angered by a cut in government funds, introduced legislation for his state to secede from the Union.

THEY REALLY *ARE* MONSTERS

The IRS would have you believe that all those stories about vicious agents are exaggerations. But that isn't what veteran IRS officers testified before Congress.

According to the testimony, the heads of district offices routinely ignore official policy and base promotions on the number of seizures agents conduct and the amount of property they seize, whether the seizures turn out to be justified or not. A sign in the Los Angeles office reads, "Seizure Fever—Catch It." Some offices offer extra time off to those who conduct the most seizures. As evidence, a memo from a Baltimore district chief was introduced it read, "The revenue officers that are performing above a satisfactory level will be rewarded, and the ones that are not will be documented with corrective actions"—this despite testimony from the IRS commissioner that he prohibits promotions based on seizures and collections.

All this testimony was taken as Congress considered passage of a "taxpayers' bill of rights." Some senators were reluctant to sign the legislation, however. As one put it, "I don't know that I want to flag myself for an IRS audit."

WAS CUSTER BLASTED AT LITTLE BIG HORN?

General George Custer had vowed to his straitlaced wife that he'd live a temperate life. However, archaeologists unearthed a large cache of champagne bottles at the homestead where Custer lived just before leading his troops to the Battle of Little Big Horn. Now they're trying to find out if Custer was a raging drunk whose fondness for the bottle led him and his troops to destruction. Stay tuned in 1988 for further word.

BOSSES FREE TO RIFLE DESKS

Be careful what you leave in your desk. A 1987 U.S. Supreme Court decision said that bosses do not need court warrants or probable cause to search their employees' offices, desks, or file cabinets.

ARE ALL WRITERS CRAZY?

A study of writers reported in *Psychology Today* revealed that 43 percent of them suffer from some degree of manic-depressive illness, compared with 10 percent of the population, and 80 percent of all writers had been treated for "mood disorders," compared with 30 percent of the population.

CRACK AND CRIME

A study by the National Institute of Justice showed that an incredible 78 percent of people arrested for serious crimes in Manhattan in 1987 tested positive for cocaine use.

FAMOUS FACES TAKE IT ON THE CHIN

For some reason, two New York plastic surgeons released a list of celebrated men whose faces, in their opinion, could use some chin chiseling. Included in the list of flawed faces were:

Rob Lowe: chin too long
Bruce Springsteen: protruding lower jaw
O. J. Simpson: overdeveloped jaws
Mick Jagger: overgrown top jaw
Senator **Ted Kennedy**: buck teeth, square face
Sylvester Stallone: underdeveloped upper jaw and cheekbone
Marlon Brando: receding chin
Eddie Murphy: underdeveloped jaws
Ringo Starr: receding chin

WORST IDEA FOR A HOME VIDEO

A Chicago-based video firm released a sixty-minute tape entitled *Inside Goetz*, a documentary that prominently features the taped statement of New York City's famous "subway vigilante," **Bernhard Goetz**.

TALK ABOUT A MUDSLINGING CAMPAIGN...

For fourteen years, the folks in Fallbrook, California, have been deciding who gets the honorary position of mayor in a unique fashion—a real mudslinging contest.

This year it was Pearl Marsh, age sixty, and Robert Olds, thirty-four, who stood back to back, paced off six steps, then turned to fire salvos at each other from their own specially prepared buckets of mud. Marsh put up a good fight in the duel, which was conducted at high noon. But Olds's special mud preparation was soupier, and he managed to cover his opponent completely before she mucked him up. Olds was declared the winner in what strikes us as the most sensible form of dirty politics.

UNITED KINGDOM OUT

Longleat, England, July 28
A pride of lions attack a pair of tailor's dummies at Longleat Safari Park, west of London, during a demonstration. Park authorities were warning the public not to leave their cars while visiting animals in the enclosed area.

4.
WHAT A WAY TO GO

WE ALL HAVE TO GO sometime, but some of us leave in a more bizarre manner than others. Take twenty-three-year-old Amy Beth Champion, for example. She was drinking in a restaurant with her thirty-year-old boyfriend and his father. She got into an argument with them and ran from the restaurant into the dark, rainy night. A few minutes later, the boyfriend, Mark Ingham, and his father decided to go look for her. They started driving down the road—then ran over her and killed her as she lay in the road. The Boulder, Colorado, police announced that no foul play was suspected, and no one had the slightest idea why Amy had decided to lie down on the road.

In contrast, an unfortunate subway clerk who suffered a massive heart attack in his underground token booth was in the headlines for the circumstances after his collapse. In a story not destined to improve the reputation of New York City, a subway passenger apparently attempted to buy a token, then noticed the clerk's body. So he scavenged a metal bar from the subway platform, pried open the locked door to the booth, and robbed it, getting away with over $1,000 in cash and some transportation tickets. This ghoul evidently then hopped the turnstyle, caught the next train, and went on his way.

We've collected more stories of the bizarre and ghoulish in the pages that follow. Hope they don't give you nightmares.

HANDYMAN OF THE YEAR

Albert Robinson of West Leyden, New York, was using a crowbar to unclog his snowblower. The next thing he knew, the snowblower had embedded the crowbar in his skull, critically wounding him.

MURDER BY REPTILE

Two men in Wallington, New Jersey, were charged with attempting to kill a neighbor by slipping three timber rattlesnakes into her apartment. The woman came home from work, opened her apartment door, and saw a venomous rattler coiled and ready to strike. A neighbor rushed to her aid and killed the snake with a baseball bat. The terrified woman confronted two other snakes before arresting the upstairs neighbor, who had complained that she was excessively noisy.

A twelve-year-old Long Island, New York, boy was killed when his head became trapped in the power window on the tailgate of his family's Jeep Wagoneer. The youngster was installing a CB radio in the Jeep when the window accidentally started to close.

HAIR TODAY, GONE TODAY

April 29

Don Lyrek is shown before and after his recent meeting with "Hour Magazine's" master of makeover, Joseph Eber. The 30-year-old Lyrek, from Rockford, Illinois, had let his hair grow unchecked for 15 years, before allowing Eber to make the first cuts.

In Mesa, Arizona, police were called in when the bodies of Mike Rywant, age sixteen, and John Sosa, thirteen, were found floating in a backyard pool. An investigation revealed that the cause of death was sniffing Freon, the gas used as a refrigerant in air conditioners.

In Detroit, twenty-nine-year-old Michael Wimbush was charged with first-degree murder after he used a kitchen blender to stab and beat to death his aunt.

Dorothy Humphrey of Detroit, Michigan, was charged with the murder of her three-year-old daughter. To punish the little girl for wetting her bed, she beat the child, then shoved her into a running washing machine, where the girl drowned.

DEATH BY WATERBED?

In Brooksville, Florida, Karl Hall was enraged when his wife Betty came home with a new hairdo. So he allegedly slashed their waterbed and tried to drown her by holding her head inside. Betty's thirteen-year-old son saved his mother's life by beating Karl over the head with a walking stick.

PRESS CONFERENCE OF THE YEAR

Pennsylvania State Treasurer **Budd Dwyer** held a press conference to protest his innocence after a bribery conviction. Then, with dozens of still and video cameras pointing at him, he pulled a revolver out of an envelope, stuck it in his mouth, and blew his brains out in front of the huge crowd.

FATAL MISTAKE OF THE YEAR

In Verona, Italy, a twenty-nine-year-old truck driver murdered his two-year-old daughter and his pregnant wife, then committed suicide, all because he was convinced he had contracted AIDS. His doctor told police the man had the flu.

DON'T TEMPT THE GODS

A prominent Bossier City, Louisiana, attorney, Graves Thomas, stood on the deck of his new boat, raised his hands, looked up at the sky, and for some reason called to the Lord, "Here I am." Although there had been absolutely no sign of an electrical storm, a lightning bolt came down from the clouds and struck Thomas dead.

THE STRANGEST CELEBRITY MURDER

Susan Cabot-Roman, a 1950s B-movie star and a former companion of **King Hussein** of Jordan, was allegedly murdered by her son, a twenty-three-year-old dwarf. The Los Angeles police arrested the son and charged him with beating his mother to death with the steel shaft from a dumbbell. The son had told police that a burglar dressed in the robes of a Japanese Ninja warrior had knocked him unconscious and murdered his mother.

IT WASN'T CUPID'S ARROW

Two men were having a violent argument on a Baltimore, Maryland, street. One fetched a hunting bow, notched an arrow, aimed, then warned an innocent bystander, a woman who was nine months pregnant, to get out of the way. Unfortunately, the man didn't wait for her to move. She was slain by the arrow. Her unborn baby was removed by Caesarean section but later died of respiratory problems.

MECHANICAL MURDER

Killer robots have murdered at least ten Japanese workers in the last eight years. In a number of cases, the robots just started working, reaching out their mechanical arms and killing workers. No record if they said they were sorry later on.

WRONG PLACE FOR A NAP

A sleepy man in Oceanside, New York, picked the year's worst place to take a nap—right under the front wheels of a huge tractor-trailer in the parking lot of a truck stop. Sure enough, the driver soon started up the tractor and backed up, squashing the sleeper.

BAD IDEA

In West Monroe, Louisiana, suspected cocaine dealer Thomas Bradley figured he'd escape charges by swallowing a half-ounce of coke when his car was stopped by police officers. He didn't go to jail—he died.

REVENGE OF THE NINJA

Breaking up can be hard to do—and lethal. Eustache Rodriguez, age twenty-two, of Brooklyn, New York, evidently took rejection very hard. He confronted his ex-girlfriend, eighteen-year-old Johane Mentor, on a street and knocked her to the ground. Then he pulled out a five-foot-long samurai sword and cut her head off.

MURDER AT SEA

Iranian forces weren't the only danger for U.S. sailors in the Middle East. On the aircraft carrier *Constitution*, which carries a crew of five thousand, sailor Martin Sturdy was struck on the head with a wrench, robbed, stabbed, and then tossed into the Arabian Sea. Charged with his murder were two shipmates, who may have been angered by Sturdy's efforts to collect $1,500 he'd won in a poker game.

HE DIED SHOOTING THE BULL

In Harrisville, West Virginia, Donal Ahner, a county prosecutor, was butted 50 yards along the ground and killed when he tried to use a needle to vaccinate his 2,500-pound prize bull.

TRAGIC GUILT

William Dowling, age fifty-two, was driving down a busy street in Land O'Lakes, Florida, when nine-year-old Jennifer Carr dashed in front of him. According to eyewitnesses and police, there was absolutely nothing Dowling could have done to avoid hitting the girl. After the girl was struck, Dowling leaped out of his car to attend to her. Jennifer was badly but not fatally injured. Dowling, however, was so grief stricken that he went home, pulled a 9mm. pistol from his gun case, and killed himself.

NO LAUGHING MATTER

Randall Jack O'Dell, age thirty-two, and his wife, Shanna, thirty-one, were found dead on their waterbed by their children. Next to them was a tank of nitrous oxide gas—known as "laughing gas."

MURDER BY TRUCK

Truck driver Kenneth Metzler, thirty-three, was thrown out of the Benchwarmer Pub & Eatery after an argument with his girlfriend, a waitress at the Indianapolis, Indiana, establishment. A few minutes later, he returned—behind the wheel of his 24,000-pound truck, which he slammed into the restaurant at full speed. One woman was killed and eighteen were injured.

WHOOPS!

In Stockton, Missouri, Cedar County Sheriff C. A. Larew was shot to death by a booby-trap device set to deter burglars.

THE VET PROTESTS TOO MUCH, METHINKS

Vietnam veteran S. Brian Wilson joined other demonstrators protesting arms shipments to Central America. To dramatize his protest, he kneeled down on the railroad tracks outside the U.S. Naval Weapons Station in Concord, California, to stop a munitions train.

Unfortunately for Brian, the munitions train didn't stop, and he was hospitalized in critical condition.

MOOSE OPINION

August, Maine, February 11
A person dressed up like a moose expresses his opinion while listening to testimony at a hearing before the Legislature's Inland Fisheries and Wildlife Committee. A bill was introduced to expand by 50 percent the annual kill during moose-hunting season.

5.
IF YOU THINK YOU'VE GOT TROUBLES . . .

A LOT OF PEOPLE who end up embroiled in scandal aren't scheming politicians or career criminals; they're just plain folks who use a little bad judgment or are the victims of bad luck. Since all of us are guilty of an occasional indiscretion that gets us into a little trouble, it makes us feel better when we read about people who end up in a lot of trouble.

One such unfortunate was thirty-six-year-old Marian Snyder of Nutley, New Jersey, a successful New York fashion buyer. Miss Snyder's problems began with an unidentified married man who was her lover. It seems that this guy's sexual fantasy was to rape a woman in a car in a parking lot. Miss Snyder agreed to participate. So they evidently drove to a "park and ride" lot in New Jersey. There the man stripped Snyder naked, tied her up, superficially slashed her with a knife, and fulfilled his sexual fantasy.

Then came the problem. The plan was that Snyder would free herself from her bonds and drive home. But she was tied too tightly. A passerby saw her struggling and called police.

Embarrassed, Snyder made up a story about being slashed and raped by a long-haired man with a mustach. Police launched an elaborate investigation and assigned men to shadow Miss Snyder for two weeks. From the beginning, however, they had doubts about her story. Her wounds were superficial, and her description of the suspect was a composite of the appearance of the two detectives who took her statement. Eventually, the cops confronted her, and she admitted the story was a lie. She was charged with filing a false police report, and Hudson County filed suit to collect from her the $10,000 they had spent on the investigation and police protection. The only person who escaped was her boyfriend —Snyder loyally refused to tell the cops who he was.

Other cases of bad luck can have more serious consequences. One such incident involved a highly respected fifty-eight-year-old Episcopal minister, the Reverend George Charles Hoch, who had a parish in Brooklyn, New York. Hoch had served the parish for twenty-eight years, and through savings and shrewd investments had become a millionaire. Unbeknownst to his congregation, however, Hoch was also a homosexual. One day late last summer, Hoch picked up a blond young man in a gay cruising area of Atlantic City, New Jersey, and drove him to his summer home. The young man spent two days at Hoch's house. On the morning of the third day, he used an electrical cord to strangle the naked priest in bed. Then he stole the priest's wallet and credit cards and took off. The police who investigated the crime believe the priest had the bad luck to pick up a suspected serial killer who may have killed as many as forty men all across the country.

A lot of the stories that follow don't have such unhappy endings. Most of them will make you say to yourself, "I'm glad that wasn't me."

TALK ABOUT SPECTACULAR EXITS

Roger Lane loved his motorcycle, so he and his bride, Mary Jo, decided to use the bike for a dramatic getaway from the church after their wedding. Problem was, half a

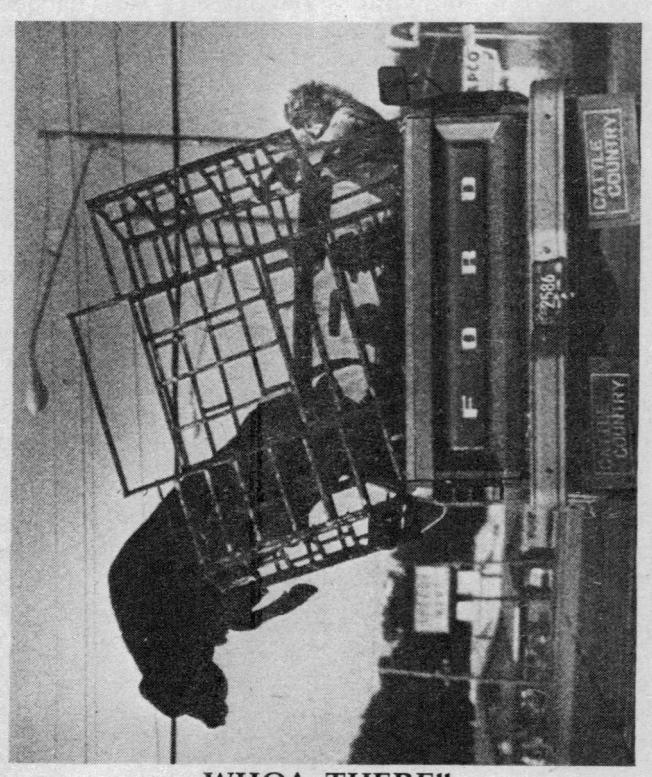

WHOA THERE!!

Coffeyville, Kansas, May 21

That's what Janet Hurley said when a rambunctious bull decided he wanted out of the Hurley pickup truck on a ride home from the stockyards. Mrs. Hurley's husband Tony had to stop the truck at a local park where the bull was held in a pen used during the city's annual rodeo. (John Davis) block from the church Mary Jo's wedding gown got tangled in the rear wheel, and the bike crashed.

Police had to use hydraulic tools to free Mrs. Lane's arm, which got caught in the spokes when she tried to free her dress. She was rushed to the hospital for surgery for a compound fracture. Her biker husband, who fainted in the emergency room, also had a broken arm, but his injury was less serious.

A BLAST FROM THE PAST

Songs tell us that "breaking up is hard to do." But most women who break up with a man don't have as many troubles as twenty-four-year-old Hermione Pierre of Queens, New York. After she broke up with twenty-seven-year-old Alan James, he allegedly sent her an innocent-looking pen that contained a spring-out blade, which cut her hand when she opened the package. A month later, another package arrived. As Hermione started to open it, she recognized the scent of James's favorite cologne. She pushed the parsel away as a powerful bomb exploded. She suffered cuts and a broken thumb, and her eighteen-month-old niece was blown across the room. James, described by his boss as a "deeply religious Jehovah's Witness," was charged in federal court with sending an explosive device through the mail.

GURU GOES BROKE

Investment guru **Albert J. Lowry,** the author of several best-selling get-rich-quick books including *How You Can*

Become Financially Independent by Investing in Real Estate, filed for bankruptcy in federal court. Can the millions of people who bought his books and attended his expensive seminars get their money back?

THE SCARLET LETTER, 1987 STYLE

In Portland, Oregon, Judge Dorothy Baker took a cue from the seventeenth-century Puritans when sentencing Richard Bateman, forty-seven, on two counts of sexually abusing children. She sentenced Bateman to a year in jail followed by four years on probation. During the probation, Bateman was ordered to hang signs on his house and car warning that he was a convicted sex offender. In the understatement of the year, Bateman complained that the sentence would make it hard for him to find an apartment and a job.

BUTTERGATE?

There was egg all over the faces of the members of the Vermont state dairy cooperative after it was revealed that the co-op's "Vermont" brand of lightly salted butter really comes from Wisconsin and Ohio.

AMY CARTER SPANKED

Well-publicized protester **Amy Carter,** daughter of former **President** and **Mrs. Jimmy Carter,** was kicked out of prestigious Brown University for failing to keep up with her academic work.

MONKEY SEE, MONKEY DO

A monkey being shipped from the Philippines to New York City escaped from its cage in the freight compartment of a China Airways 747 jet as it landed at John F. Kennedy Airport. The monkey soon made its way to the passenger compartment, where flight attendents rushed off the plane to avoid being bitten. Next thing the pursuers knew, the monkey was sitting in the pilot's seat, manipulating the controls as if trying to taxi for takeoff. The monkey was captured soon afterward.

SPORTS MANAGEMENT OF THE YEAR AWARD

Despite the very lucrative television contracts enjoyed by the National Football League, the *Boston Globe* reported that the Sullivan family, owners of the New England Patriots, have managed to lose over $75 million dollars since they bought the team.

ADDING INSULT TO INJURY

In Chico, California, a very unfortunate twenty-one-year-old man named Billy Bittle was rushed to the hospital for treatment of injuries suffered in an auto accident. During surgery, the poor man's operating table suddenly burst into flames, badly burning him between the thighs. Ouch.

WHO'S THAT POLISH FELLOW DUCKING OUT THE BACK WAY?

The lawyer for Peggy Cameron of Wichita, Kansas, announced plans to serve the Pope with a subpoena during his visit to the United States. The reason: Ms. Cameron bore an illegitimate son by a Roman Catholic priest and she's suing the Catholic church for damages.

TEENAGE PARTY-OF-THE-YEAR AWARD . . .

Goes to the guys and gals who trashed Vicki Cole's house in Tacoma, Washington, to the tune of $350,000 in damages. Mrs. Cole was away for the evening, and her sixteen-year-old son Gunner invited some friends in. Slam dancing soon turned into egg fights and cottage cheese fights. Soon the teenagers were setting off aerial fireworks in the livingroom. After Gunner passed out drunk, two boys sprayed a basement wall with hair mousse, deodorant, and other sprays, then set it on fire. The fire department arrived just in time to pull the unconscious Gunner from the flames.

Some of the partygoers were later summoned to face the music again, this time on charges that included arson, theft, and malicious mischief.

A federal judge in Manhattan awarded $702,044 to the family of a man who died in 1953 after the army gave him experimental doses of a hallucinogenic drug. The man, forty-two-year-old tennis pro Harold Blauer, had been admitted to a Manhattan mental hospital. Without his permission, he was injected with five doses of mescaline supplied by the Army Chemical Corps as part of an experiment to develop chemical warfare agents. The lawsuit came about after a ten-year investigation by Blauer's daughter into the cover-up of her father's death.

YUCK!!!

Officials in Minneapolis–St. Paul report that winos who live on the street have begun to drink Lysol disinfectant spray. They punch holes in the bottom of the can, drain out the liquid, and mix it with water, juice, or soda.

THE MOST EMBARRASSED LEGISLATOR AWARD . . .

Goes to the city councilman in Washington, D.C., who persuaded the council to debate his proposed bill to toughen penalties for prostitution. The bill hit a big red light when a streetwalker testifying at the hearings identified the bill's sponsor as one of her clients.

IN THE BIGGEST SHOCK OF THE YEAR DEPARTMENT

Billie Carfagno of Washington, North Carolina, spent over half a year looking for his wife, who had run away from home. When he finally found her in Las Vegas, he discovered she'd recently given birth to quintuplets. No word on whether he ran away from home.

HE'S ABOUT 10 FEET LONG, WEIGHS A THOUSAND POUNDS . . .

A night watchman at Moscow's Klin Circus and Zoo somehow managed to lose Rouseland the hippopota-

IF YOU THINK YOU GOT TROUBLES...

mus. By the time he found the beast, the hippo had wadded into the Sestra River, where it played and dived. The watchman tried to entice the animal out of the river, but its leg got caught in a drainpipe and it drowned.

The night watchman was fired, and two senior officials were reprimanded.

NOW, THAT'S A HOT LINE!

The University of Mississippi issued a press release containing a special 900 telephone number that football fans could call to hear a recorded message about the prospects for the upcoming season. However, the *Clarion-Ledger* misprinted the number by one digit. The wrong number connected fans to a service that provided a pornographic sexual message. A member of the paper's sports staff reported a lot of complaint calls—including one from a fan who wanted to be reimbursed for the cost of his call. But it turned out the guy had called the porno number five times.

THE BAD LUCK AIRLINE PASSENGER OF THE YEAR

The Executive Communications Group gave its annual Frankenstein Travel Award for the most horrifying travel tale to Robert Cole of Hartford, Connecticut. Cole was the only passenger aboard a commuter airline flight from Hartford to Boston—and they lost his luggage.

DISCRIMINATION IN SPORTS

Curious about the reasons for all the controversy over racial discrimination in sports? A survey of the eight colleges in the Atlantic Coast Conference showed that although black athletes outnumber white athletes twenty-five years after the conference was integrated,

- None of the 8 schools employed a black as athletic director or assistant athletic director.
- Only 3 of 87 head coaches were black, and only one black coached a major sport.
- Only 20 of 121 full-time assistant coaches were black.

HOSPITAL HORROR STORIES, VOLUME 1

A forty-seven-year-old retarded man was admitted to a hospital in upstate New York. The reason: his body was covered with horrible bedsores, the result of allegedly inadequate physical therapy at the state center for the mentally retarded, where he had lived since age twelve. Doctors decided that the bedsores needed massive skin grafts. To obtain the skin, they decided to amputate his legs—without obtaining the required consent from the man's sister or the courts. Before amputating the man's legs, they decided to perform a colostomy, removing much of his colon. After they inserted breathing and feeding tubes down the man's throat, he developed pneumonia and died.

JUSTICE FOR A HUSBAND

After his 1981 divorce, James Garvey was ordered to make child support payments and mortage payments on the house in which his ex-wife Mary lived. Then, in 1984, Mary hit the Massachusetts state lottery for a hefty $6.4 million. She began to live it up, buying an expensive car and homes in Florida and Vermont —while James struggled to make his support payments. In 1987, however, a judge decided that wasn't fair. He ordered Mary to pay $250,000 in alimony to James.

HOSPITAL HORROR STORIES, VOLUME 2

Doctors in the genetic counseling unit at a Long Island, New York, hospital told a pregnant woman that the drug she was taking for a gland problem had severely retarded the growth of her baby's brain. At their urging, she reluctantly had an abortion. The baby, however, was normal. It turns out the doctor counseling the woman had based his diagnosis on a dosage of the gland medication that was a thousand times greater than the amount the woman was taking—she would have had to swallow ten to fifteen pounds of pills a day to do the described damage. The woman sued the hospital and was awarded $150,000 in damages for her emotional distress.

THE SADDEST STORY OF 1987

A seventeen-year-old scuba diver became lost in an underwater cave, then scratched a good-bye message on his empty air tank before drowning. The message read, "I love you Mom, Dad, and Christian."

The young man was diving in a Florida creek marked "No Diving." He died on his mother's forty-second birthday. He had planned to go out to dinner with her that night.

HIS "FEELINGS" WERE REALLY HURT

A federal jury in Manhattan awarded a French songwriter half a million dollars in damages after deciding that the song *Feelings* had been stolen from his original work. The jury decided that Brazilian singer-composer **Morris Albert** had stolen the tune from **Louis Gaste**'s 1956 song, *Pour Toi* (For You). Ouch, that hurts!

NOW, THAT'S HEAVY EQUIPMENT

Caterpillar, Inc., agreed to an out-of-court settlement with Luanna Cashatt, who had sued the company for illegally discharging her. The company's reason for the discharge: Luanna's figure (40-20-36) was keeping men workers from concentrating on their jobs. She charged that the workers who were distracted were "the ones from the front office, the ones in suits, and they'd hang around me all the time." What was her former position? Believe it or not, heavy equipment operator.

TAX MEN GET WRONG NUMBERS

The Government Accounting Office, the investigative arm of Congress, had investigators pose as taxpayers to ask questions in calls to the IRS. Nearly one-quarter of the answers—22 percent—they received were wrong, and another 15 percent were incomplete.

JOBS GO UP IN SMOKE

The USG Corporation ordered workers at USG Acoustical plants to either quit smoking or be fired. Complained one worker, "As far as I'm concerned, it's Communism. I think it's all Communism."

IN THE WORLD OF BAD IDEAS...

A Los Angeles company called Ultraphone began a twenty-five-city telephone service called Scoopline.

Teenagers could dial a special number and be connected to as many as ten other kids to chat with.

As you can imagine, some problems emerged. One father in New Mexico came home to find his thirteen-year-old daughter entertaining a twenty-six-year-old man who had posed as a teenager on the phone to get a date and had then arrived with booze. Drug deals were allegedly conducted using the line, and profanity and sexual propositions became commonplace.

Then came the phone bills—as high as $7,000 for one teenager. One phone company, Mountain Bell in New Mexico, canceled the service.

WE'VE ALL MADE HONEST MISTAKES, BUT...

Investigators say it was an honest mistake—and a whopper. Merrill Lynch fired Howard Rubin, head of its trading department in mortgage-backed securities, after he lost an incredible $250 million in unauthorized trades. This little bundle is reportedly the largest single trading loss in Wall Street history.

IF YOU THINK YOU'VE GOT TAX PROBLEMS...

A federal grand jury indicted three executives of the bankrupt investment firm, Securities Group, for providing $550 million in false tax write-offs through fraudulent securities trading. The investors in the group—who will probably have to pay back taxes, penalties, and interest on the phony deductions—included TV producer **Norman Lear** ($1.5 million in deductions), actor **Michael Landon** ($1 million), actor **Sidney Poitier** (over $500,000), and CBS chief executive **Laurence Tisch** ($1.1 million).

PRESIDENTIAL TIMBER SHOWS ROT

Toward the end of his second term as President, **Dwight Eisenhower** remarked that he'd like to have his Treasury secretary, **Robert Anderson,** succeed him, commenting, "Boy, I'd like to fight for him in 1960!"

In 1987, Anderson, who turned to business instead of campaign politics, pleaded guilty to tax evasion and illegal banking operations. The crimes ranged from concealing income to putting an alleged girlfriend on the payroll of a company he controlled.

THE NEO-NAZI EDUCATOR AWARD FOR 1987 . . .

Goes to an Indiana high school basketball coach who punished players who performed poorly by making them wear a ball and chain to classes. Commented a psychologist at an Indiana university, "There's an awful lot of data that says positive reinforcement works better."

MOST INTRIGUING NEWS STORY

Below is an entire news story clipped from the *New York Post*:

> A woman's legs have been found in the woods behind a church near Brookville, Indiana. The legs, in blue jeans and suede boots, were cut off 8 inches above the knee.

Can anyone provide a follow-up? Who's knees were they? Tune in next year.

SOME MARRIAGES AREN'T MADE IN HEAVEN

Marital bliss lasted a matter of minutes for Thomas Mihalkc, age thirty-eight, and Ann Mello, thirty-four, of South Kingston, Rhode Island. Mihalkc allegedly went wild when his bride danced with another man at the wedding party, so he started beating her. He was arrested, but his bride later requested the charges be dropped—understandably, she's seeking to have the marriage annulled.

THERAPIST CLEANS UP

In one of the year's most sensational divorce cases, a Long Island, New York, dentist charged that his wife came under the influence of a pseudo-psychologist who had a "voodoo like" hold on her.

The whole mess began when a rabbi referred Dr. Alvin Olesh and his wife Ronni to Dr. Steven Clarfeld, a Colts Neck, New Jersey, psychologist. Clarfeld charged them $300 to $400 for weekly five-hours sessions. Soon Allen Cooper, Clarfeld's assistant, joined the sessions. Cooper, a former mental hospital janitor who had no psychological training or license, began traveling with the couple, then moved into their home.

That's when, Olesh charges, some monkey business began. He allegedly caught his wife going down to Cooper's room in the middle of the night. Ronni later visited Cooper in various motels for "therapy sessions" —which Olesh charges consisted of "hands on" therapy.

The end result: Olesh spent $25,000 on therapy and entertainment. The divorce suit is bitter, and Olesh has sued Clarfeld and Cooper for $10 million.

And what exactly was the ex-janitor's therapy technique? According to him, he has the power of "therapeutic linguistics"—the ability to make soothing singsong noises. He said, "I have mastery in the art. I am considered a wizard because I make linguistic utterances which are very therapeutic."

John Stossel, a reporter on ABC's *20/20* news magazine, received $425,000 in an out-of-court settlement. Stossel claimed he lost partial hearing when professional wrestler David Schultz, known as **Dr. D.,** cuffed him on the ears.

MORE "DO AS I SAY, NOT AS I DO"

The subject of the panel discussion was freedom of speech. But one of the panelists, Dr. Victor Herbert of the Mount Sinai School of Medicine in New York City, became enraged when he discovered one member of the audience was tape-recording the discussion. He was arrested after rushing down from the stage and seizing the cassette tape.

FISH CATCHES BOY

A five-year-old boy was knocked unconscious and hospitalized after a 250-pound brown-spotted ray leaped out of the Gulf of Mexico and landed on him. The boy recovered, but his father said, "It was quite bizarre . . . almost like a nightmare come to reality." No word on the condition of the fish.

GOVERNMENT WORKERS GET THE BLUES

In order to prevent federal employees from cheating when asked to produce urine samples, the government announced that "toilet-bluing agents" will be placed in all stalls to prevent workers from taking samples from the bowl. The head of the National Treasury Employees Union blasted the move, calling it "a comic exercise in Ty-D-Bol justice."

EDUCATION BOO-BOO OF THE YEAR

Talk about embarrassed. The California State Bicentennial Commission made what Governor **George Deukmejian** called "a very major mistake" when it sold a textbook in which black children were referred to as "pickaninnies."

On the surface, it might seem unfair to the mother that the Tennessee Court of Appeals ruled that Hal Warden didn't have to pay her $30 a week in child support, as ordered by a lower court. But, you see, Warden happens to be a sixteen-year-old tenth grader, who also happens to be the twice-divorced father of two children. The Court of Appeals recognized that Warden's only income was a $15-a-week allowance from his father, so it suspended child support payments until he was out of school.

By the way, the father of the very precocious teenager

announced that Hal "has no plans of dating any girls or getting married to anybody now."

GOOD IDEA, BAD WARDROBE

James Lee Heighton, twenty-five, of Santa Monica, California, had a great idea—he'd dress in women's clothing, walk into the women's locker room of a local health club, and film women in various stages of undress.

Unfortunately, his disguise wasn't the best. On the sound track of the tape seized by police, a woman's voice is heard remarking, "Did you see that guy wearing a bra and wig?" A female employee called the cops, and Heighton's undercover filmmaking days were brought to an abrupt end.

SIGN OF THE TIMES

Daisy Manufacturing announced it will put orange stripes on its BB guns to identify them as toys. It seems a lot of teenagers were using the guns to pull stickups.

YES, IT'S TRUE, BOB

The U.S. Supreme Court upheld a lower appeals court

ruling that overturned a $1.6 million damage award to *Penthouse* magazine publisher **Bob Guccione**. Guccione had sued the competing men's magazine *Hustler*, which published an article that called him an adulterer.

The Supreme Court, however, pointed to the fact that Guccione had openly lived with his girlfriend for thirteen years while he was still married, and thus was in fact an adulterer, even though he was divorced by the time the *Hustler* article appeared. The nation's highest tribunal thus ruled that after thirteen years of "living in sin" Guccione was "libel-proof" on the subject of adultery, even though he resented seeing the term in print.

OOPS

In Pangburn, Arkansas, forty-seven-year-old Jim Hiburn stopped his car by the side of a mountain road and got out to admire the view. Only thing was, he failed to notice that he was on the edge of an unrailed cliff —his first step took him 260 feet down, and he was killed.

YOU DIRTY RAT ...

An off-duty police officer in Detroit shot himself in the shoulder while trying to kill a rat that had attacked him in his garage. The officer tried to shake the rat off his shoulder, but was unsuccessful. Then he shot at it—but hit himself.

WAITING FOR JOAN

Beverly Hills, California, July 16

Peter Holm, estranged husband of actress Joan Collins, awaits her return to her Beverly Hills home with signs in hand referring to his ouster from a home they shared nearby.

6.
SCANDAL AROUND THE U.S.A.

IF YOU READ THE gossip columns and watch the network news, you're likely to think that Washington, D.C., Manhattan, and Hollywood have a near monopoly on scandal. But the truth is that misbehavior isn't copyrighted. The same temptations that lead movie stars and politicians into trouble tug at the conscience of people all over America, in small towns as well as big cities from coast to coast.

A lot of news stories seem more scandalous when you consider where they took place. For example, Miami, Florida, has a well-publicized problem with violent crime, especially drug-related violence. That's why it would seem that the Miami criminal justice system should have better things to do than to arrest a woman for feeding a hungry baby. A Miami woman was traveling with two pre-school children on the city's public transportation system when her eighteen-month-old asked for something to eat. She opened a tin of sausages for him—and was promptly arrested for violating a rule against eating in public. Fortunately, a judge threw out the arrest—but not before the city of Miami suffered yet another blot on its reputation.

Some stories are made more amusing because of their

regional flavor. For example, those of you who follow politics know that the first important delegate selection for the 1988 political convention takes place in Iowa. That's why the Great Midwestern Ice Cream Company decided to name some flavors after presidential candidates. Midwestern dessert fanciers have their choice of Bush's Peppermint, Du Pont Super Rich Fudge, Dole Top Banana, Robertson's Born Again Chocolate, and our favorite (but not Gary Hart's), Donna Rice Cream. We're sure voters are amused, but we hope the ice cream's not as hard to swallow as some of the political rhetoric.

Speaking of flavors, we hope you'll find some delicious scandals in the following stories selected for their local flavor.

Sullivan County, New York

New York State Attorney General **Robert Abrams** filed suit to dissolve the Sullivan County Society for the Prevention of Cruelty to Children. The reason: The group was allegedly formed solely to allow members to carry pistols without permits. Under the current law, members of child protection groups are considered peace officers, and as such, they can legally carry weapons.

The attorney general, however, discovered that not a single member of the Sullivan County group lived in Sullivan County. The organization's telephone number was an answering service, which reported that no one had checked for messages for months. The group had never investigated a single case of child abuse.

TRY WALKING THIS STRAIGHT LINE

Jamestown, New York, September 17

These lane dividers on West Eighth Street are not the result of a tipsy painter. Nor are they meant to trap drunken drivers. Made of tape, they are the result of movements of the earth unter the roadbed.

Montpelier, Vermont

The number of prison inmates convicted of sex crimes in the state has tripled in just six years, according to state officials. Are they putting something in the water?

Media, Pennsylvania

Poodle owner Harvey Moskowitz became incensed when Labrador retriever Rex, owned by a neighbor, allegedly scratched the ear of his beloved dog. Moskowitz grabbed a knife, went next door, pushed his way inside, cornered Rex in the basement, and stabbed him to death.

Judge Robert Kelly sentenced Moskowitz to four to twenty-three months of weekends in jail for this "shocking" crime. He also ordered Moskowitz into counseling.

Queens, New York

The executive director of the Flushing, Queens, Boys Club, the 1985 Flushing Rotary Club Man of the Year, was arrested by the FBI for sexually abusing a fifteen-year-old Boys Club member whom he'd taken on a vacation trip to Mexico.

Lockport, New York

In settlement of a lawsuit, the South Lockport Volunteer Fire Company agreed to pay $1,600 in damages to Rodger Schermer, who was denied membership in the company because he wore Scottish kilts. Looks like firemen don't like knees.

Buffalo, New York

Mayor James Griffin named an investigator to probe the theft of $52,000 from a softball league run by the Common Council. Question of the year: How did a softball league get $52,000?

Dedham, Massachusetts

A jury awarded $610,000 in damages to Susan Murphy. She claimed that the International Society of Krishna Consciousness intentionally ruined her relationship with her mother while Susan was a member. What price would you set for your relationship with your mother?

Staten Island, New York

We've heard of people camping out on the steps of City Hall. But an anonymous Staten Island resident found a better way to get the attention of the borough president, a position similar to that of mayor in other cities. This person must have known that Buddy, the borough president's cat, liked to wander a bit during the day. One day Buddy returned home bearing a note around his collar, addressed to his owner. The note read: "There's a big hole in the street on City Boulevard, near Herkimer Street. Please have it repaired before I fall in." Guess what? The pothole was fixed the next day.

ENDICOTT, NEW YORK

The outraged owner of Brendle, a purebred English springer spaniel, filed a paternity suit against her next-door neighbor, owner of a mutt named Bo. In the suit, Brendle's owner charged Bo with unlawful lovemaking that resulted in the birth of eight mixed-breed puppies. She said the illicit liaison prevented a planned match with another purebred springer spaniel that would have produced puppies worth $150 apiece. The owner's asking for damages—plus, we presume, puppy support for the unwed mother.

Plymouth, Massachusetts

In the town where the Pilgrims landed in 1621, an 800-year-old Indian village was ruined by a bulldozer that accidentally plowed up the site while clearing ground for a housing development.

Westchester County, New York

In a year in which the weapon of choice for most indicted investment bankers was a telephone, one prominent financial man got in trouble using a gun. **Arthur Salomon**, of the famous investment banking family, allegedly got into an argument with a nineteen-year-old college student after a close call on the highway. After a short argument, Salomon allegedly went to his car, took out a gun, plugged the college student in the stomach, and drove away. He was later arrested and charged with attempted murder.

Maple Shade, New Jersey

Maybe the cops were nervous because of all the publicity about the freeway shootings in Los Angeles. In any case, the cops swarmed all over thirty-eight-year-old mechanic Allan Davis. His crime: squirting a water pistol into another driver's car during an argument. Davis was hauled into the slammer and charged with aggravated assault for "wantonly pointing a firearm, manifesting extreme indifference to the value of life." If squirt guns are that deadly, why doesn't Rambo use one?

Leominster, Massachusetts

It was a "cat-astrophe"—but at least Screamer the cat lived up to his name in the end. Gilbert Cabana was cat-sitting for Screamer, the pet of his son's girlfriend when, at 5:00 A.M., Screamer decided to do a little wandering. He pulled a window curtain down onto the burners of an electric stove, then walked on the pushbutton controls, turning on two burners. Then he went into Cabana's bedroom and started screaming.

Cabana woke up—in time to see his kitchen going up in flames. He and the cat escaped; the house suffered $30,000 in damages.

Dover, Delaware

Although it completely ruined his chances to become State Legislative Leader of the Year, Representative William Oberie, Jr., resigned as State House GOP leader after being chided about his behavior—which included drinking beer on the House floor and carrying a pistol into the Capitol.

New York, New York

It wasn't a good year for formerly prestigious New York Hospital. First came criticism from a grand jury over "woefully inadequate care" in the death of **Libby Zion**, daughter of writer **Sidney Zion**. Then came a report from the New York State Health Department, pointing out errors that may have contributed to the death of **Andy Warhol**. Finally, on a night in June, the hospital's maintenance staff shut off the power to make some repairs. A few minutes later, the backup generators failed, shutting off the respirators that were keeping fifteen premature babies alive. Doctors and nurses rushed to keep the tiny infants breathing—but one died.

Worcester, Massachusetts

Despite a state law banning the sale of tobacco products to minors, an eleven-year-old girl was able to purchase cigarettes in seventy-five out of one hundred stores she visited as part of a research project.

Katonah, New York

All she did was ask a little favor, and for that she got whacked with two to six years in jail. What was the favor? Robin Spadaccia, thirty-one, asked her first husband to lend her $2,000—to pay hit men to kill her second husband. The first husband, who was probably very glad to be an ex, turned her over to the cops.

New York, New York

For fifty years, Julian Altman played his violin at society affairs in New York and Washington. On his deathbed, he made a confession to his wife: The violin was a Stradivarius, worth as much as $1 million, which he had stolen from a Polish violinist in 1936. His widow gave the violin back to its rightful owner, Lloyds of London, the insurance company that had paid the Polish violinist $30,000 after the loss.

Albany, New York

On the eve of the city's Tulip Festival, vandals cut the blooms off more than twelve thousand tulips. A $5,000 reward was offered for the capture of those responsible for nipping the celebration in the bud. An Albany television station reported that it had received a call from a woman who claimed the act was committed by an organization she called the "Albany Tea Party," which was protesting tax hikes.

Hancock, Massachusetts

An angry farmer announced that he was going to stop paying a $100 fine every time one of his sheep or cows wandered into a neighboring nudist colony. The farmer, who complained that the nudists' cars spooked his animals, paid $5,000 in fines and $70,000 in legal fees between 1976 and 1986. The case marked the first time animals ever had to pay to see naked people.

Homer City, Pennsylvania

John and Lisa Shields were indicted on charges of involuntary manslaughter in the deaths of their two small children, whom they had left in a blazing-hot locked car with the windows shut for five hours.

Someone was allegedly so incensed by the children's death that he or she set the Shieldses' house on fire the night of their arrest. Neighbors came out to see the blaze—and cheered.

Norfolk, Virginia

Joanie Staggs, age twenty-two, was sentenced to sixty days in jail for abandoning her baby daughter in a motel room. Seems the baby's crying was keeping her boyfriend awake. So the couple moved to another motel, leaving the annoying baby behind.

Baltimore, Maryland

The state Planned Parenthood group offered a Valentine's Day gift that was very, very "now"—although not classically romantic. The gift: a heart-shaped box containing five condoms, a poem about condoms, and a pamphlet explaining their use.

Boston, Massachusetts

Police announced that prostitutes arrested in Boston would get all of their property back when they were released from custody. The statement came after prostitutes complained that the cops were refusing to return the condoms the hookers carried as protection against AIDS.

Spotsylvania, Virginia

Poor Christine Bond, age fourteen. She'd just settled in for a good night's snooze on her waterbed—when an empty car crashed through the wall of her bedroom and pinned her to the mattress. It took twenty minutes to get her loose from the alien auto, which had slid down the street while warming up in a neighbor's driveway.

West Babylon, New York

John Baker, age forty-four, hadn't been able to find a job for ten years, and evidently the frustration finally got to him. Police stopped his van one night and found a thousand marbles, a high-powered slingshot, and a BB gun. John had allegedly used these weapons to break windows at the offices of a thousand companies on Long Island over the course of a year.

Montevallo, Alabama

Day-care workers "forgot" a little nineteen-month old boy who was one of the regular passengers in a van that picked up tiny tots and brought them to a day-care center. When the locked van was reopened after six hours in the sun in 91-degree heat, the little toddler was dead. Said Sheriff J. F. Glasgow, "There's got to be some kind of criminal negligence in a case like this."

Shelby, Kentucky

AMONG THE WORST JUDICIAL DECISIONS . . .

The Kentucky State Supreme Court reversed the conviction of Mary Knox of Shelby, Kentucky, ruling that she broke no law when she allowed her husband to rape their daughter.

Elizabethton, Tennessee

Forty-one-year-old Noe E. Campbell insisted on a trial to prove his innocence on a drunk driving charge. To prove his charge that the blood-alcohol testing device didn't work properly, he drank four beers in the courtroom. The device worked perfectly, so Campbell had two headaches the next morning, including a conviction.

Shreveport, Louisiana

They gave an election but nobody came. Officials sat around the Dixie Garden Civic Center polling place all day, but not a soul voted. It seems that only two eligible voters lived in the entire precinct. Neither one of them showed up because, according to the election commissioner, if they had, "everyone would know how they voted."

Portsmouth, Virginia

The city attorney found the fingerprints of Mayor James Holley II on hate mail sent to community leaders who were opposed to the closing of a local high school.

Hodgenville, Kentucky

Talk about a story that leaves a bad taste in your mouth—Hodgenville residents were told to boil their drinking water after 100,000-plus gallons of liquid manure leaked into the river that supplies the town's tap water.

Houston, Texas

Call it poetic justice. Texans love to brag about being the "biggest and best," but what they created last year was the biggest commercial flop of the year. Sales of souvenirs for the state's much-ballyhooed 150th birthday reached only 4 percent of projections, leaving embarrassed Texas merchants with over $100 million in unsold and useless junk.

Weston, West Virginia

To remove weeds from around a riverbank tree, Weston Mayor Danny Whelan bought Bill E. Goat for $5. When the Humane Society saw poor Bill E. tied to the tree, they went to court and got a warrant for Whelan's arrest on charges of cruelty to animals. Bill E. is a free goat while the case is in the courts.

Altamonte Springs, Florida

An eight-year-old scientist found an error in an educational workbook produced by Harcourt Brace Jovanovich, a giant textbook publisher. The third grader pointed out to the publisher that its question, "What planet has rings?" is wrong, because two planets have rings, Saturn and Uranus. The publisher sheepishly agreed to mend its ways.

San Antonio, Texas

Texans have a reputation for shooting from the hip, but the gunmen seem to be getting younger. A mother in this Texas city saw her four-year-old son playing with Daddy's shotgun. She frantically tried to disarm him, but he fired, wounding her in the hip. Bet she's happy Daddy left his shotgun lying around.

Malvern, Arkansas

A teenager performing a handstand on the hood of a moving pickup truck was killed when he fell off and hit the pavement. Police blamed the movie *Teen Wolf* for starting the fad of doing handstands on moving vehicles.

Fort Lauderdale, Florida

Theresa Jackson, age forty, was arrested on charges of aggravated child abuse, procuring sexual performances by a child, and forgery after the suicide of her beautiful seventeen-year-old daughter, Tina. Jackson allegedly steered her daughter into nude go-go dancing, then forged her birth certificate to make her two years older so she could get a job. The mother allegedly drove her daughter to and from work, then demanded much of her pay. The young girl shot herself in the mouth with her mother's revolver after an argument with her mother over moving out.

Moody, Alabama

Vicki Elmore was charged with second-degree assault after she spanked an assistant principal with the same paddle the school administrator had used to punish her first-grade son.

Louisville, Mississippi

The Winston County *Journal* used to give an award to the first baby born each year, but merchants who donated the prizes objected when the 1986 winner was an illegitimate baby. The paper changed the name of the contest to the "First Legitimate Baby of 1987 Contest." It turned out that the paper had to wait until January 10 and give the award to the fourth baby born in the county in 1987.

Miami, Florida

A bag containing an estimated $400,000 fell off a Wells Fargo armored car on I-95 one Thursday afternoon. Evidently, the accident caused a great deal of civic concern, as more than one hundred motorists thoughtfully stopped to help Wells Fargo by collecting some of the stray cash. Unfortunately, those same motorists thoughtlessly neglected to give the cash back to the armored car company.

Falmouth, Kentucky

Most of us get mad at banks every once in a while. That's probably why a jury acquitted Wilbur Costigan, who was charged after attacking three bank computer terminals with an ax. Costigan was frustrated about some debts; the jury evidently figured those computers deserved what they got.

Homer, Georgia

The Garrison family of this small town of 750 people hid 132,100 Easter eggs—72,000 hens' eggs, 60,000 candy eggs, and 100 prize eggs—on its 40-acre farm.

Hattiesburg, Mississippi

In what must have been one of the least popular campus visits of the year, Jim Gilles, a self-proclaimed "missionary to American college campuses," announced that the University of Southern Mississippi was a "cesspool of lust." He added that some of its "wild women" wore clothing that said, "Rape me." He gave one coed a copy of a book he had written, signing it with these good wishes: "Repent, you cigarette-sucking sinner."

Gulfport, Mississippi

Mrs. Dorothy Tucker called police to report that her baby was lost. It turns out that the absentminded Mrs. Tucker had made a whopper of a mistake. She and her mother had set the two-month-old on top of the car while putting another child in the car—then they forgot about the baby and drove off. A half-block later, the baby slid off the roof, breaking a collarbone and suffering scratches and bruises. Mrs. Tucker drove several more blocks before she realized the baby was missing.

Tampa, Florida

Two eleven-year-old boys charged with kidnapping and raping a nine-year-old boy were charged as adults. The reason: at their tender age, the two had more than twenty criminal counts on their records.

Parchment, Michigan

An American Civil Liberties Union official charged that the Parchment Board of Education was acting unconstitutionally in requiring boys and girls to wear graduation gowns of different colors. What the ACLU failed to state was, who cares?

Coral Gables, Florida

Evidently, Tommie Hines got so absorbed in beating his wife with a tire iron that he left some valuable evidence behind when he fled. The evidence: his artificial right leg. Police put out a description of the fugitive, who was described as wearing "a white and red shirt, blue pants, one red and white sock, and one black shoe."

Macon, Georgia

IS THIS THE OFFICE OF DR. DRACULA?

Workers arriving for the day in offices on the top floor of the sixteen-story Charter Medical office tower found dozens of dead and dying bats all over the place.

Hillsboro, Alabama

Talk about lousy jobs. If the turnover rate is any indication, being a member of the two-man police force of this town must be one of the worst jobs around. In just two years, the town has had six police chiefs and eighteen police officers—the average officer stayed on the job just six weeks.

Houston, Texas

A jury deliberated on this grave situation, then awarded $142,000 to a couple who were extremely upset when they learned that their $74,000 home was built on an old graveyard. But the jury also decided that the builder didn't deliberately deceive the couple, so they refused to award an additional $2 million sought by the homeowners.

Dallas, Texas

After years of battling thieves who bashed in parking meters to steal the change, Dallas authorities finally decided to end the problem by purchasing three thousand tamperproof meters at $175 apiece. The results: The thieves started taking the entire meter; they walked off with over fifty in the first two weeks.

Houston, Texas

A judge ran out of potential jurors for an assault trial—so he sent deputy sheriffs to a downtown shopping mall to pick up shoppers for jury duty.

The justification for the action was the state's "round-up law," which dates back to the 1880s, when circuit-riding judges had to round up citizens before they could hold court. The deputies came back with fifty-six decidedly unhappy citizens.

Cape Canaveral, Florida

A forty-two-year-old woman sneaked into the U.S. Air Force rocket base next to the Kennedy Space Center and climbed atop a thirteen-story tower used to launch spy satellites. To back up her charge that this base had "no security whatsoever," the woman explained that she had to call base security twice before they came to the tower to arrest her for trespassing.

Bryan County, Texas

The county government finally quit paying a $7.50 bounty for wolf ears, after learning that no wolves have lived in the county for ten years. Seems enterprising citizens were collecting on German shepherd and coyote ears. Shame on them.

Pensacola, Florida

Thieves shoplifted a box of condoms from a convenience store. When the manager gave chase, they turned around and started shooting—they must have really needed protection.

Norfolk, Virginia

Passengers nearly panicked when they smelled fuel in the cabin of a People Express jet, so the pilot made an emergency landing. Turns out the odor came from the pants of a passenger who said he slipped and fell into a puddle of fuel while walking out to the aircraft.

Fort Worth, Texas

The owner of three Texas companies that claimed to help locate missing children was arrested on charges of defrauding customers of $182,000.

Nashville, Tennessee

Salomon Wingfield, age thirteen, was among students sent home from school early because of a snowstorm. When he opened the front door, his father mistook him for a burglar and shot him.

Columbia, South Carolina

Some Columbia residents gave the city a real black eye one night when they refused to help a twenty-six-year-old woman who had been repeatedly raped by five men. After the woman managed to escape her attackers, she ran naked from door to door in a middle-class neighborhood pleading with someone to let her in—but absolutely no one opened the door or called police. The men recaptured her, then raped and beat her again. Finally, she escaped a second time and found a man who let her in and called authorities. No word on exactly how many people should be thoroughly ashamed of themselves.

Casselton, Iowa

The best birthday blast of 1987 might have been the surprise cooked up by Janice Irby for her husband John's thirty-first. John had asked for golf balls and a birthday cake, so Janice decided to put the golf balls in the cake mix. After a few minutes in the oven, the cake exploded.

Des Moines, Iowa

Driving while "loaded" is bad enough if you're behind the wheel of a car. But it's a lot worse if you're hauling a truckload of radioactive waste. State troopers charged Richard Beirau with driving under the influence of alcohol after his load of 50,000 pounds of radioactive wastes slid into a ditch—nearly ensuring that half the state would have a "glow on."

Chicago, Illinois

Like many bosses, first-term Chicago Alderman Wallace Davis, Jr., expected loyalty in a secretary—even after he'd been indicted on several corruption charges. When his former secretary testified before a grand jury, he decided to enforce loyalty—by allegedly pistol-whipping her.

Oshkosh, Wisconsin

Heard of May-December romances? Well, in the small town of Utica, outside of Oshkosh, there was a

November-January romance. The district attorney's office was investigating the case of a nineteen-year-old woman who was pregnant by a twelve-year-old farmboy. Seems the two coupled in a hay mound on the farm of the boy's parents. Officials were deciding whether to prosecute the woman for sexual assault. Even if they do, the boy's parents are liable for the child's support.

Kansas City, Kansas

Despite the fact that eight students were treated for heat-related illnesses from sitting in non–air conditioned classrooms during a record heat spell, the compassionate school board suspended two dozen students for wearing shorts to school. Seems that wearing shorts violates the dress code, while passing out is perfectly legal.

South Bend, Indiana

The theory of more-is-better took a new twist when Mary Cecilia Alford and Jeffery Andre Diggins exchanged marriage vows. Their wedding party numbered a whopping fifty-six attendants—nineteen bridesmaids, nineteen groomsmen, two maids of honor, two best men, three matrons of honor, three attending groomsmen, two flower girls, two ring bearers, one junior bridesmaid, one junior groomsman, and two ushers. What's a junior bridesmaid?

Wichita, Kansas

Dr. Gran Evans, sixty-five, a retired gynecologist, wrapped himself in a sheet and burned himself to death in a hospital bathroom. The 1987 Crime Detection of the Year Award candidate, Fire Chief Bruce Roberts, deduced, "Evidently, he was kind of despondent."

Wyandotte, Michigan

Wyandotte gourmets had to postpone a new taste experience when the State Health Department persuaded restaurant owner Johnny Kolalowski to take his newest dish—muskrat—off the menu. The Health Department had to determine whether muskrats were safe to eat. Yum, yum, can't wait to taste roast rodent.

Boise, Idaho

Few crime victims have the presence of mind of a young woman who was raped in this Idaho city. While the rapist had his mind on other matters, the victim picked his pocket, snaring his wallet—with I.D. inside. The police quickly nabbed the alleged criminal, twenty-two-year-old Stuart Duaine Robinson.

Columbus, Ohio

No parent-of-the-year honors for Lorene Smith, a thirty-two-year-old mother of two boys, ages three and five. Acting on a tip, police entered her apartment to find her calmly watching television—while on two separate beds rested the decomposing bodies of her two children. Smith was indicted on murder charges.

Kansas City, Missouri

Fans of the teenybooper Latin group Menudo were surprised when a member of the group's band died of an accidental drug overdose before a scheduled performance.

Williamson, West Virginia

The mayor ordered a public swimming pool closed for cleaning after discovering that a carrier of the AIDS virus had been swimming—despite assurances from state health officials that the AIDS virus cannot be spread in swimming pools, especially in water containing chlorine.

Next we'll hear about a mayor who ordered citizens to

stop breathing after an AIDS carrier walks through town.

Smith Center, Kansas

Retired seventy-five-year-old body shop owner Star Barron was arrested for pumping forty-five bullets into a replica of the Statue of Liberty. Barron had been arrested on the same charge for the same crime—thirty years before.

Joliet, Illinois

Robert Harrison, a former Chicago disc jockey, and his wife, Deborah, pleaded guilty to aggravated criminal sexual abuse of their fifteen-year-old baby-sitter. The charge involved their providing the girl with drugs and alcohol, then having sex with her on at least two occasions.

Duluth, Minnesota

Trucker Robert Benson was sleepy, so he pulled off the road to take a nap. When he woke up, he found himself floating down the St. Louis River. The extremely surprised driver rolled down a window, crawled out, and waded to shore while his rig disappeared downstream. Police said the truck had rolled down the riverbank while Benson napped.

Green Bay, Wisconsin

To 1,100 folks attending the Toby Tyler Circus, the big top turned out to be a big flop. In the middle of the performance, the tent collapsed on top of the entire audience—just seconds after the tigers had finished performing and were safely back in their cages. Forty people were injured.

A year earlier, sixty-six circus-goers had been injured when wooden bleachers collapsed at a Toby Tyler show. The circus also allegedly had accidents in Pennsylvania and Ohio, and a New York investigation found the circus didn't have insurance.

Midland, Michigan

Auburn Hudson had a bad day. As usual, he walked out of his house in the morning, picked up the newspaper from his lawn, hopped into his car, and started driving to work. Problem: There was a live bird inside the newspaper. Hudson, who wasn't wearing his seat belt, stopped the car to let the bird out. But somehow the car kept rolling and he fell out.

Hudson started to chase after the car, but his pants fell down. Hobbling with one leg in his pants and one leg out, he saw the car roll farther and farther away, then crash into his neighbor's house.

Hudson spent the day at Midland Hospital being treated for minor injuries—and, no doubt, saying, "Why me?"

Redwood City, California

A woman immediately removed herself from consideration for "mother of the year" honors when she was sentenced to twenty-eight years in jail for pimping for her fourteen-year-old daughter, forcing the girl to perform oral sex and unlawful intercourse.

San Francisco, California

Wallaby's restaurant, which features Australian food, decided to feature kangaroo meat on the menu. The decision boomeranged, however, when animal rights groups picketed the eating establishment. The restaurant had to yank its special from the menu when authorities pointed out that it was against California law to import kangaroo carcasses.

Phoenix, Arizona

There were some red faces when guards at Arizona State Prison discovered two bottles of wine cooler and a can of beer in a van carrying three members of the

Pardons and Paroles Board into the correctional facility. The members of the board may be reviewing their own sentences—carrying liquor into a prison is a felony.

Boulder, Colorado

In a possibly precedent-setting case, a seventeen-year-old girl sued her family minister for improperly counseling her. When the girl told the minister that she was a victim of incest, he told her to pray, instead of counseling her to report the crime to authorities.

Bend, Oregon

Thirty-five-year-old James E. Luttrell, former pastor of the Bible Baptist Church, was sentenced to ten years in prison for sodomizing and sexually abusing a six-month-old baby boy.

Los Angeles, California

Hot times in the hot tub landed Los Angeles motorcycle cop Kelly (Clickety) Klatt in hot water. Klatt, the most prolific ticket writer in the department, was suspended and charged with misconduct after a twenty-four-year-old woman charged that she traded a speeding ticket for a couple of nude dips in the hot tub with Klatt and his partner.

Palm Springs, California

A homosexual was granted custody of the sixteen-year-old son of his male lover, who had died of AIDS. The court denied custody to the fundamentalist Christian mother of the boy, who had twice been accused of kidnapping him.

Indio, California

A wild chase between police and a man accused of stealing a bakery truck ended in a pie fight. Cornered after four miles, the thirty-seven-year-old man decided to make a last stand. He began heaving freshly baked pies at officers, who hurled pieces back. Police reported no injuries, but several officers were "severely stained."

Los Angeles, California

We've heard of turning a deaf ear, but the tenants of an L.A. apartment building must have set a new record.

They ignored a sixteen-year-old girl who screamed for six hours while she was gang-raped in an apartment by eleven men.

Fullerton, California

The coaches of the Sunny Hills High School basketball team were suspended after abandoning six members of the team by the side of the road in the desert after a road trip loss.

Federal Way, Washington

Just give me some of that rock-and-roll music and I'll kill you any old way I choose it . . . That might have been the motto of thirty-six-year-old Daniel Patrick Lynam. His murderous rampage was discovered when neighbors peered into the window of his parents' house to discover why rock music had been blaring for two days. Lynam had murdered his parents at their house, traveled to the condo of his wife's parents to dispatch them with .38 caliber gunshot wounds to the head, then gone home to kill his wife, his five-year-old son, and his two-year-old daughter. Lynam was still alive when the cops came to his house, but when they broke in ten minutes later, they found that he'd killed himself—the eighth and last victim of his rampage.

West Covina, California

Doctors surgically reattached the ear of a seven-year-old boy after it was recovered from the stomach of the dog that had bitten it off.

Roslyn, South Dakota

Somebody in the Hauge family of Roslyn has some explaining to do. You see, a New York City surveyor found the Hauge family photo albums and other family documents in a trash can on a Harlem street. Isn't it fun to think about what they were doing there?

San Jose, California

A woman filed a $500,000 lawsuit against the San Jose *Metro*, claiming damage to her reputation after the paper ran a picture of the lower half of her bikini-clad body, along with a caption that mentioned casual sex. The editor of the paper retorted, "There was nothing to identify her, unless someone could identify her belly button."

Salem, Oregon

TALES OF THE HEARTLESS

The Valley Credit Service of Salem, Oregon, seized the life savings of four-year-old Sean Russell—a total of $18.28 the little tot had saved from birthday gifts. The collection agency was trying to collect for unpaid bills resulting from Sean's daddy's heart surgery.

Anchorage, Alaska

The Alaska Continental Bank gave away handguns to people who agreed to deposit $10,000 for three years at 4 percent interest. Now, that's robbery.

Fargo, North Dakota

A federal judge ruled that Frances Warner has the legal right to seek damages from four state officials who participated in the decision to fire her from her job as a drug counselor because she had used the drug peyote. The grounds for the challenge? Warner is a member of the Native American Church, which has approval from the U.S. Congress to use peyote in its religious rituals. Take that, you state officials, you.

Boise, Idaho

For decades, Idaho license plates have carried the inscription "Famous Potatoes." Now a citizen of Boise is suing the state to have the slogan removed, charging that it unfairly discriminates against other Idaho products.

Mesa, Arizona

David and Carolyn Hubbard won a $4.5 million settlement in a suit against Sears. The couple charged that a Sears garage-door opener caused brain damage to their five-year-old daughter.

Arvada, Colorado

A judge ordered Janice and Alfred Bryant to jail because their daughter missed forty-three days of school and was late nineteen times in one semester. The daughter was ordered to spend a month in a detention center. Do you know where your children are today?

Denver, Colorado

The stuffed animals at the Denver Museum of Natural History are being devoured by vicious carpet beetles.

Los Angeles, California

L.A. is movieland, but Michael and Wendy Glover didn't appreciate a home that looked like the set of **Alfred Hitchcock's** famous movie, *The Birds*. When the couple switched on the light in their den, they discovered the walls and furniture blanketed with two thousand swifts, which had swooped down the chimney during the night.

Los Angeles, California

Ex-pro football lineman **John Matuszak** has gotten movie and TV roles as a crazy tough guy. His latest real-life act got him five days in an L.A. jail. Seems that Matuszak went slightly berserk after a traffic accident. He tried to rip the door off the other guy's car, then punched him.

Warden, Washington

Biggest disappointment of the year to all you reptile fans is that Dave Estep's attempt to set a record by crawling into a sleeping bag stuffed with 250 rattlesnakes will have to wait until 1988. Local residents managed to come up with only 100 rattlers for the attempt. The current record for crawling into a sleeping bag stuffed with rattlesnakes is 224.

Gilroy, California

Gilroy high school seniors had planned to sell about 500 copies of a calendar as part of a drive to raise money for a trip to Disneyland. Then came the decision to include pictures of female students clad in bikinis. The print run zoomed to 2,000 copies.

Juneau, Alaska

State Senator **Mitch Abood** triggered a fierce argument in the state legislature when it was considering a resolution asking Congress for highway funds. The resolution referred to Alaska's "harsh environment."

Abood argued that words like "harsh" are damaging

to Alaska's image and its tourist industry. Ignoring the fact that the temperature outside the building was 45 degrees below zero and the wind was blowing at 40 miles per hour, Abood suggested substituting the phrase "unique environment" for "harsh environment." He further argued that no legislative bills or resolutions should mention the words "snow" and "cold."

No word on whether the legislature argued that Christmas should come 365 days a year.

Santa Ana, California

Mary Jo Jansen, age forty-four, walked into a classroom at a local elementary school, where twenty-seven fifth grade students were sitting. Entering through a rear door carrying two handguns, she walked up to the teacher and announced, "Sorry I have to do it this way."

The teacher immediately realized the woman intended to kill herself. She pleaded with Jansen not to take her life, asking the class, "Do you students want this woman to live?"

The students all yelled, "Yes, Yes!" But Jansen proceeded to shoot herself in the head.

Moran, Wyoming

Authorities were on the watch for a particularly vicious varmint—a seat-eating coyote. Seems the four-legged beast wandered into Charlie Walker's snowmobile rental place and chewed up the vinyl and foam seats on fourteen snowmobiles—presumably because of the food scents left by tourists.

Oklahoma City, Oklahoma

A teenage girl was charged with felony cruelty to animals for allowing forty-two purebred Persian cats to starve to death while her mother, a cat breeder, was hospitalized in Houston, Texas. The girl actually lived with the carcasses of some of the animals for more than a week before she was arrested.

Provo, Utah

A twenty-four-year-old man drove his car through the glass doors of the Utah State Psychiatric Hospital, stopped at the switchboard, jumped out, and told the panicked operator, "I'm going crazy and I need help."

The operator didn't know what to think. The police thought the guy was faking. They hauled him off to jail for criminal mischief.

Muskogee, Oklahoma

Austin Walker, a Cherokee Indian, was so broke he was living in a car. But his circumstances changed abruptly when a federal judge awarded him $685,000 after ruling he'd been cheated out of leasing rights to gas and oil on his land. The judge blasted the Bureau of Indian Affairs for allowing an attorney to represent Walker who was also representing the oil company that had offered the Indian $4,000 for the drilling rights to his land. It turned out that substantial gas and oil had been pumped from Walker's land before the oil company took the trouble to sign him to the deal.

Rancho Cucamonga, California

On a spring night, several teenagers were playing laser-gun tag in a dark schoolyard. Unfortunately, someone called the cops and reported prowlers at the school. When the cop arrived, nineteen-year-old Leonard Falcon jumped out from behind a building and fired a beam of light at him, evidently believing the cop was one of the players.

The cop thought he was being fired at. After a second flash of laser light, the cop blasted Falcon with his shotgun, killing him.

Reno, Nevada

Like many other citizens, Elizabeth Smith had long watched the antics of politicians and decided they were "mixed up" and "didn't do very much." Unlike a lot of citizens, she decided to get involved and run for mayor. So she went down to the city clerk's office and filed papers, which listed her age—a ripe 102.

7.
SCANDAL AROUND THE WORLD

SCANDAL IS AN INTERNATIONAL preoccupation, and 1987 was a wonderful year for misbehavior abroad. A most interesting foreign scandal was revealed last year when an old letter was discovered, which was written by French King Louis XV in 1749. It seems the king suffered from a very modern problem—he wanted to enjoy the pleasures of his mistresses without fathering a lot of potentially troublesome illegitimate heirs to the throne. He saw a possible solution when he heard that condoms were being made in England from sheep bladder and intestines. The king sent a letter to the Duke of Cumberland, asking "to procure from England, as it is not a manufacture of this country, 300 or more of those preventive machines made use of by the gallant tho' prudent young gentlemen of this age."

Another scandal of a different sort resulted when a New Zealand woman with a drug habit was caught with 4.9 ounces of heroin on a trip to Malaysia. It seems that the criminal justice system in that Far Eastern country is a little more strict about drug possession than the courts here in the States, where dealers are usually back on the streets hours after an arrest. This unfortunate forty-four-year-old woman was tried and sentenced to death. Her son, who had an ounce of heroin, was sentenced to life in prison and six strokes with a cane. Don't you wonder how such sentences would affect street life in our big cities?

On the lighter side, the international press had a field day as a thirty-seven-year-old Italian porn queen, Ilona Staller, successfully ran for election to the Italian parliament. Staller, known for her sizzling live sex performances in Rome's pleasure palaces, displayed scanty clothing as well as a scanty knowledge of the issues, but she won her seat. Unfortunately, the authorities weren't pleased; they started shutting down theaters and nightclubs in which she was scheduled to appear. Guess they just don't have a sense of humor.

Your funny bone, however, is likely to be tickled by some of the worldwide scandals we've collected.

Yongin, South Korea

A cult leader known as Benevolent Mother and thirty-one disciples took drugs and strangled themselves in a murder-suicide pact. The woman, Park Soon-ja, forty-eight, was under investigation by police for allegedly swindling $8.7 million from 220 of her followers. So she and 31 others hid in an attic. Clad in pajamas, some of the victims stuffed tissue paper in their noses and mouths to suffocate themselves, others donned rubber gloves to strangle one another, and some took drugs. The last man alive hanged himself.

Nottingham, England

Why was fifty-five-year-old grandmother Kathleen Campbell in the news? She became Britain's oldest

HEAVY TRUNK AND BAGGAGE

Munich, West Germany, August 18

Jopa, a 29-year-old elephant at the Munich zoological garden, Hellabrunn, is unceremoniously hoisted by a crane from the trench surrounding the elephant enclosure. It seems that Jopa got into a dispute with one or more of the zoo's other elephants, and in the resulting turmoil, fell into the moat.

mother by giving birth to her seventh child. Her other children range in age from sixteen to twenty-two.

Rio De Janeiro, Brazil

Gone are the days when hardened prison inmates spent weeks filing a spoon into a deadly weapon. Over 110 inmates in a women's prison in Rio de Janeiro used a far more deadly and available weapon—two inmates infected with AIDS. The leaders of the riot captured a prison director and held him hostage, threatening to infect his blood if their demands weren't met. Prison authorities eventually agreed to give the rioters immunity from punishment and conduct hearings on their grievances.

Back in the USSR

Last year we carried a story about exploding television sets in Leningrad. This year, the problem spread to Moscow. In the new spirit of openness in the Soviet Union, a government economist admitted in print that every 4 minutes, 42 seconds, a color TV set explodes into flames in Moscow.

Moscow, USSR

Readers of *Pravda*, the Communist party newspaper, nearly keeled over when they read the first page of a January 1987 issue. A five-paragraph article revealed that the head of the feared KGB had announced the firing of a senior KGB officer for, of all things, human rights abuse. It seems that the senior official, A. Dichenko, had jailed a journalist who investigated sloppy administration in Dichenko's district, a city in the Ukraine. There's been no confirmation of the rumor that Ralph Nader has been hired as *Pravda* columnist.

Tokyo, Japan

In the first six months of 1987 alone, the presidents of nine major Japanese firms—including Mitsubishi Corporation, Seiko Instruments, Fuji Electric, and All Nippon Airlines—died. A Tokyo psychologist attributed the high death rate to stress caused by the high yen, trade problems, and corporate restructuring. Who said the Japanese were so philosophical?

Victoria, British Columbia, Canada

The military loves to put on a show for the public, but the seventy-fifth Esquimalt Tattoo got a little out of hand. An overly enthusiastic demonstration of hand-to-hand combat led to the superficial stabbing of Private J.B.D. Gilchrist. The soldier, startled by the injury, fell, struck his head, and died.

London, England

The owners of Volkswagens in Great Britain are furious about the popularity of the Beastie Boys, a raunchy New York rap group. The reason: Group member Michael Diamond wears a chrome VW logo on a chain around his neck. So fans of the group are roaming the streets ripping the ornaments from the grills of any Volkswagen they can find.

Moscow, USSR

In an unprecedented show of public emotion, a courtroom full of spectators leaped to their feet and applauded when a woman was sentenced to just five years' probation for killing her husband with a hatchet. The reason for the enthusiasm: The woman's husband was an alcoholic who often violently abused her and her family. Just before the slaying, the deceased had threatened his wife with the same hatchet. Alcoholic domestic violence is reportedly a very serious problem in the Soviet Union.

London, England

Prime Minister **Margaret Thatcher** asked the U.S. government to waive diplomatic immunity in a case involving the husband of a woman reportedly employed by the CIA. The man, Pentecostal minister James Ingley, Jr., allegedly exposed himself to a six-year-old girl, then showed her pornographic videotapes while she was undressed.

Madrid, Spain

NOW, THAT'S BULL!

A storm of protest erupted when *El Paia*, the nation's leading newspaper, released a poll indicating that soccer had replaced bullfighting as Spain's favorite sport.

Yarmouth, Nova Scotia, Canada

MERRILY THEY STROLLED ASHORE, STROLLED ASHORE . . .

It wasn't exactly your normal morning in this small fishing village, where the only visitors are a few tourists. One July day last year, however, the residents looked out their windows to see a whopping 174 foreigners wandering their streets—173 men, most of them bearded and wearing turbans, and a woman. When one resident recovered from the shock enough to ask a visitor what he and his friends were doing there, the man asked where he could get a taxi to Toronto—1,700 miles away.

The police later discovered that the foreigners were Sikhs who had left India by boat nearly two months before. The ship's captain, who was later arrested, had dumped them in the darkness in Nova Scotia without telling them where they were. The bewildered refugees were taken to a Canadian Air Force base. The town of Yarmouth is still buzzing.

Seoul, South Korea

For some unexplained reason, the Associated Press reported worldwide a poll of South Korean children that revealed the tots ranked "mother" first on a list of ten favorite things. But "father" was only the third favorite, finishing behind "a serving of beef." Huh?

Moscow, USSR

THE MOST EMBARRASSED COUNTRY AWARD OF 1987 . . .

Goes to the **Soviet Union**, whose vaunted air defenses were penetrated by a nineteen-year-old West German youth who flew a light plane 580 miles from Helsinki, Finland, to Moscow, buzzed the Kremlin, and landed smack in the middle of Red Square. This young daredevil had a mere twenty-five hours of flying time under his belt when he defeated the massive Soviet military.

When the young man landed, a Western diplomat predicted, "Heads are going to roll." A day later, they rolled. The Soviet defense minister and the head of the Air Defense System were both canned. The rest of the world got a gigantic chuckle.

Tehran, Iran

THE AYATOLLAH JUST CAN'T TAKE A JOKE

Iran threatened to break off diplomatic relations with Turkey after *Akis*, a Turkish magazine, published a cover depicting the sour old fanatic surrounded by naked women. The Turkish government quickly apologized.

Puerto Vallarta, Mexico

IT'S A DRUG BUST, CHARLIE BROWN!

The officials at the Puerto Vallarta airport seized an airplane owned by the mother-in-law of *Peanuts* creator **Charles M. Schulz** because she had been misidentified as a suspected drug smuggler. Although the seventy-four-year-old woman and her seventy-seven-year-old female co-pilot protested their innocence, the extremely efficient Mexican police and U.S. Drug Enforcement Administration took four days to straighten out the snafu. Good grief!

Pisa, Italy

In case you've been keeping track, the Leaning Tower of Pisa leaned another fraction of an inch in 1987. That makes a total of 16.8 feet of movement since the tower was built in 1173.

London, England

SERMON OF THE YEAR

An English preacher, giving a funeral sermon, described the deceased as "a very disagreeable man with little good in him, who would not be missed."

Kwangtung Province, China

Pornographic movies made a spectacular, but illegal, debut in southern China in 1987. On February 6, 1987, two men used a videotape machine at the state-run TV transmission station to watch a porno movie entitled *The Massage Girl*. But somebody hit the wrong switch, and the movie was broadcast to the entire province. It was twenty minutes before the authorities discovered what was happening on the boob tube. We hope the two men enjoyed the show—we suspect it will be a few years before they'll enjoy female company again.

Stafford, England

Most prospective bridegrooms end up in the bag at their bachelor parties—but not as literally as a man who arrived at the Stafford railroad station at 3:00 A.M. one night. Police called to the station found a man "well wrapped up in a plastic bag, wearing brown paper and string and sporting a red star." (British Rail operates a Red Star express parcel delivery service.)

Police discovered the chap was so intoxicated he hadn't realized he'd been shipped on a train until he got to Stafford. What happened to him? Whoever put him in the bag had thoughtfully provided a return ticket, so the unflappable British authorities put him on another train and shipped him back to London.

Roding, West Germany

DEFECTION OF THE YEAR

A thirty-nine-year-old Czechoslovak engineer eluded two military jets and flew to safety in West Germany.

His vehicle—a motorized hang glider that he had spent several years building in a secret location. This enterprising freedom-seeker managed to travel 28 miles in his contraption, just beating the two jets to the border.

London, England

FOWL BEHAVIOR

Score one for management. An office worker lost a lawsuit against his employers after he was fired. The reason for the dismissal: When the ex-employee felt overworked, he had the habit of rising to his feet, flapping his arms, and loudly clucking like a chicken. The judge agreed that the worker was "quite unsuitable to deal with the public."

Toronto, Canada

IS CANADA A FEMINIST UTOPIA?

Fortune magazine dug up a study that it called the "most fascinating single social-science finding of the latter twentieth century"—if it's true. It was a Canadian government study of how women have been portrayed in television programming. Over a thirty-year period, researchers examined thousands of shows to see how many contained characters that said or did anything derogatory to women.

Now the astounding finding: The report said that since 1965, a period of twenty years, "not a single episode derided notions of sexual equality." This means that out of thousands and thousands of shows, not one single character said anything bad about women.

So, all you feminists, it's time to move to Canada, apparently the home of perfect sexual equality.

Bangkok, Thailand

Would-be rapist Boonchai Sirithanyarat figured he had an easy target when he saw a college coed walking alone down a dark street—until she opened her purse and brandished a 6-foot python she kept inside. Complained the criminal, "What kind of woman carries a python in her handbag?" A woman who expects to meet up with creeps like you, that's who.

London, England

ROYAL FAMILY SECRETS

The *Star* newspaper of London revealed that two of **Queen Elizabeth's** first cousins, whom the British directory *Burke's Peerage* listed as long dead, had in fact spent decades as patients in a mental hospital. The two women, Nerissa and Katherine Bowes-Lyon, daughters of the brother of the Queen Mother, were born severely retarded. Although *Burke's* recorded the death of one sister in 1941 and of the other in 1961, the *Star* learned that Nerissa died in 1986 and that Katherine was still alive.

Warsaw, Poland

When a Polish LOT jet plunged into a forest south of Warsaw, killing 183 people, a small army of looters were among the first people to arrive on the scene. While medical personnel looked for survivors, the looters stole rings and money from the bodies of the victims.

Lhasa, Tibet

A hotel was fined $135 for bringing tourists to the site where corpses are hacked into small pieces and fed to vultures as part of the local custom of "sky burial." No doubt you'll want to change your vacation plans now.

Tokyo, Japan

A Buddhist monk who's a combat veteran of World War II charged that American soldiers took home as souvenirs the skulls of one thousand Japanese soldiers who died on Iwo Jima. He's demanding the return of the skulls, out of consideration for the families of the dead.

Ottawa, Canada

The Canadian government is considering building at least ten nuclear attack submarines to keep both the Soviet Union and the United States out of Arctic waters. Commented External Affairs Minister **Joe Clark**, "The larger threat to our sovereignty in the North comes from our friends . . . the United States."

Lagos, Nigeria

Traditionally, Nigerian fathers have controlled their daughters' destiny, primarily because marrying them off to men who can pay dowries can be lucrative. However, when two fathers pulled their daughters out of college to get married, the government stepped in. A judge ruled that the country needed college graduates badly, so pulling the young women out of college for personal gain was unpatriotic. Both fathers were jailed for a year.

Australia

Many Australians' dreams came true when 675 automatic teller machines at branches of the Westpac Bank started spewing out millions of dollars in cash.

Japan

Many Americans are angry about our huge trade deficit, but the Japanese wondered if the R. J. Reynolds Tobacco Company was taking it out on them. In 1987, Reynolds exported to Japan 160 million cigarettes that were contaminated with herbicide. Are the Japanese going to send us some exploding television sets in retaliation?

Huarmey, Peru

An accident on the coast highway proved dangerous for people miles away. A bus collided with a truck. Eighteen people were killed, twenty-two were injured —and lions, tigers, panthers, and monkeys escaped from the truck and took off for parts unknown. Police said an undetermined number of circus animals were unhurt, and had taken the opportunity to return to nature.

London, England

It seemed like a good plan. Andrew Greene, nineteen, decided to rob gas stations clad in nothing more than a stocking mask, because he didn't want to be identified by his clothes.

Well, it didn't work—witnesses identified the teenager by his physique, vaccination marks, and skin blemishes. The court ordered Greene to undergo psychiatric evaluation.

Peking, China

The Canton Cultural Bureau banned entertainers from wearing bikinis, saying they were "obscene and vulgar." The only Chinese allowed to wear bikinis were female bodybuilders.

London, England

Being thirsty isn't a crime—but being too thirsty after a crime can be extremely hazardous. Robber Darren Bullen knew that video cameras had caught him robbing a bank, and he'd planned to go right home after the crime to change his appearance and dye his hair. But he felt really dry and gave into the temptation to stop in a pub for a beer. Unfortunately, he was sitting right next to an off-duty policeman when films of his robbery were broadcast on TV. The policeman made the arrest without getting off his bar stool, and Bullen was on his way to six years in jail.

Broome, Australia

Where was Crocodile Dundee when they needed him? Ginger Meadows, twenty-four, a vacationing Colorado model, was killed by a crocodile while swimming off a luxury cruiser moored in the Prince Regent River in one of Australia's wildest areas. Searchers finally found her body on a riverbank, put it in a body bag, then shipped the body on a small boat so it could be taken to the nearest city. While the boat was steaming downriver, a large crocodile leaped four feet out of the water and closed its giant jaws around the body bag. The crew of the ship managed to fight off the croc.

Swansea, Wales

The Royal Society for the Prevention of Cruelty to Animals denounced the annual fund-raising event of this small village as "cruelty to shellfish." The event: cockle tossing. Handfuls of the small bivalve mollusks are put into socks and tossed across a field.

Jerusalem, Israel

The Orthodox Jewish mourners at the Mount of Olives cemetery were solemnly preparing to bury a male

Orthodox Jew. So imagine their surprise when they opened the casket to find the body of a woman, who also happened to be wearing a Christian cross around her neck.

Dacca, Bangladesh

Pandemonium reigned in Dacca Medical College Hospital when five poisonous cobras suddenly appeared in a packed third-floor ward. At least fifty patients ran screaming from their beds before hospital workers killed the snakes. Snake charmers were called in to stand guard in case more cobras were lurking.

Manila, Philippines

Cardinal **Jaime Sin**, archbishop of Manila, announced that he believed prayers by four priests had "softened the hearts" of the kidnappers of a Japanese businessman, who was released after 137 days in captivity. When reporters asked if the cardinal thought the $3 million ransom paid by a Japanese firm got the businessman his freedom, the prelate snapped that the $3 million wasn't a ransom but "a contribution" to cover the kidnappers' costs of abducting and holding the man. Hummmm.

8.
BOY, IS THAT DUMB!

LET'S FACE IT, there are more than a few people walking around who are little more than dim bulbs. Some of them inevitably turn to crime, and when they do, the results can be hilarious.

Take the chap who got the great idea to break into police headquarters in Pittsburgh, not once, but six times. Not content with challenging fate, he happened to find a Polaroid camera during one of his burglaries. To see if it worked, he turned the lens on himself and snapped a self-portrait. Not realizing the photos took some time to develop, he tossed the negative into a wastebasket. The next day, the cops had a perfect photo of the guy who'd been rifling their desks and lockers, and he was in custody before he could say "cheese."

Some of the dumbest moves of 1987 were made by people well educated enough to know better. Take the case of Walter Atlee, the top drug abuse official of the state of California. Atlee had allegedly been engaging in illegal behavior and was on trial on charges that he'd extorted money from people who sought licenses to open methadone clinics. Now, you and I would be on our best behavior in court. Atlee, however, staggered into the courtroom one day three hours late and very drunk. The judge promptly threw him in the slammer, so "we'll know where he'll be."

Other kinds of stupidity can have much more tragic results. One example from last year is the story of the Medicaid officials who decided they wouldn't pay $700 a month for a piece of medical equipment needed by a nineteen-month-old baby in Staten Island, New York. The baby had a rare condition called apnea, which caused her suddenly to stop breathing several times a day. The Medicaid officials were hauled into court to defend their refusal to pay for the monitor, and their argument was shattered before any testimony was taken when the little girl suddenly stopped breathing, the monitor sounded, and two paramedics saved her life. The baby had no less than ten attacks during the court proceedings—but the bureaucrats still refused to budge until the court changed their minds for them. Now, that's dumb.

Below is a choice collection of some of the dumbest things people did in 1987, as well as some of the foolish things they tried to put over on people like us. Reading these tales will no doubt make you feel a whole lot smarter.

MOUSE TROUNCES MAYOR

Channel 5 television in New York City pulled episodes of the British cartoon *Dangermouse* off the air so it could broadcast a regular talk show starring Mayor **Ed Koch**. Dangermouse fans were furious, so a poll was conducted to see if the citizens were more interested in the mouse or the mayor.

Well, the result was a landslide. Dangermouse, "the

CURIOSITY SEEKER

Chambersburg, PA, July 10

A beagle puppy walks onto the scene as members of the Letterkenny Army Depot Special Reaction Team simulate a hostage rescue operation.

British Secret Service's most dashing rodent," trounced the mayor by a whopping 10 to 1 count.

IN THE DUMBEST GOVERNMENT REPORT DEPARTMENT . . .

Omni magazine reports that a government-funded study of why pizza burns the roof of your mouth concluded that the tomato sauce is very hot. We can't wait for future studies telling us that apples grow on trees and the sun shines during the day.

KODAK TURNS UGLY

Kodak, by far the largest financial contributor to the University of Rochester, New York, bullied the school into giving the heave-ho to a student who happened to work for **Fuji Film**, Kodak's big rival.

HOW DOES THIS COMPARE TO YOUR BUDGET?

In the course of his divorce proceedings, **Peter Holm** asked for a modest $80,000 a month temporary support from his wife, actress **Joan Collins**. Below is the "bare bones" budget he submitted to the court:

Household Expenses

Rent	$16,500
Household salaries	$7,000
Payroll taxes	$1,400
Household cash	$300
Groceries	$1,900
Household supplies	$2,500
Utilities, telephone, cable	$2,570
Dry cleaning	$100
Insurance	$300
Security	$200
Total household	$32,170

Car Expenses

Leased BMW	$7,295

Other

Club membership	$400
Newspapers and magazines	$100
Personal grooming	$200
Medical expenses	$250
Gifts	$1,650
Audio supplies	$400
Computer equipment, supplies	$3,000
Freight, messengers	$100
Office expenses	$1,125
Books	$280
Clothing	$12,000
Photos	$800
Entertainment	$6,000
Cash draws	$8,000
Travel and lodging	$4,000
Other	$786
Other total	$40,591
GRAND TOTAL	**$80,056**

BOY, IS THAT DUMB!

THE DUMBEST RAPIST

In Atlantic City, New Jersey, a man repeatedly raped a woman—after she showed him a medical card identifying her as a victim of AIDS.

WE'VE HEARD OF LEAVING YOUR PRINTS AT THE CRIME SCENE, BUT . . .

Police in Lincoln, Nebraska, arrested four burglars for breaking into the offices of the Nebraska School Activities Association. It seems these brilliant criminals couldn't resist taking time from their looting to make prints of their faces on the photocopy machine. After no doubt admiring their work, they tossed their pictures into the trash can for the police to find.

IN THE RIDICULOUS GOVERNMENTAL DECISIONS DEPARTMENT . . .

County officials approved changing the name of the Rochester–Monroe County (New York) Airport to the Greater Rochester International Airport, despite the fact that no international flights take off or land there.

Complained a local resident, "You can't even fly nonstop to New Orleans."

THE DUMBEST CUSTOMER OF THE YEAR...

Has to be the guy who set off a little Bluebird firecracker while standing in Mr. W's fireworks stand in San Antonio, Texas. The little firecracker flew into a box of larger firecrackers, and a moment later $26,000 in fireworks blew up the entire stand.

YOUR TAX DOLLARS AT WORK

The Correction Department of the state of Virginia announced that it was spending the money to air-condition the death chamber in the state penitentiary to make it "more comfortable for everybody." Does that include the guy sitting in the electric chair?

THE WRONG POT GOT SCRUBBED

Two teenagers in Rome, Georgia, forgot to remove their $30 stash of marijuana when their car went through the car wash. When they got the car back, they discovered their pot had been sucked up by the giant vacuum cleaner. When the car-wash workers wouldn't open the vacuum cleaner for them, they left, then returned with wire cutters to break into the cleaning machine. They got their pot back—just before the cops picked them up.

Kansas state officials commissioned an advertisement, to be placed in national publications, that would boost the state's image. The ad, which urged people to "open their eyes" to Kansas, featured a sixty-story building reaching into the sky. Those same officials soon canceled the ad after a storm of public ridicule. You see, the state's tallest building has only twenty-two floors.

IN THE TRUTH-IN-PACKAGING DEPARTMENT

Federal officials claimed that an Idaho winery owned by the family of Senator **Steven D. Symms** charged $2 more a bottle for wine that was labeled as Idaho-grown —when the grapes really came from other states.

LOW-TECH AWARD OF THE YEAR...

Goes to the company that makes Magic Slates, those erasable plastic boards normally used by little children.

The U.S. government bought up a big batch for use by congressmen and other officials inspecting the bug-ridden new U.S. embassy in Moscow. Said a company spokesman, "We're not often called upon to serve our country's defense."

A DUNCE CAP FOR AMERICAN TEENS

How is our educational system doing? Worse than ever, according to recent surveys of sixteen- to eighteen-year-olds. Among the examples of ignorance revealed by the surveys:

- 25 percent of teens thought **Franklin D. Roosevelt** was president during the Vietnam War.
- 10 percent thought **Peter Ustinov** was leader of the Russian Revolution.
- Two-thirds couldn't date the Civil War within fifty years, and half couldn't date World War I within fifty years.
- 75 percent didn't know what the Reconstruction was and couldn't identify either **Walt Whitman** or **Henry David Thoreau**.
- 50 percent didn't know who **Stalin** and **Churchill** were.
- 33 percent thought **Columbus** discovered America after 1750.

BOY, IS THAT DUMB! 223

DIAMOND IN THE ROUGHAGE

An elderly woman offered her yardman a nice cold soft drink on a hot day—forgetting that she'd put her $3,500 diamond ring into that particular glass for safe-keeping. Sure enough, he swallowed the jewelry. After an X-ray confirmed the yardman had ingested the ring, he and the elderly woman sat around waiting for time —and the ring—to pass.

THE EFFICIENT EXECUTIVE OF THE YEAR AWARD . . .

Goes to Teamsters Union President **Jackie Presser**, who sent a letter congratulating New York Senator **Daniel Patrick Moynihan** on "his well-deserved election victory"—five years after the election. Referring to the recently revealed information that Presser has been an informant for the FBI, Moynihan commented, "If he can't get this straight, what does he tell the FBI?"

TWELVE-YEAR-OLDS IN THE GUTTER?

Some sixth graders in Brandon, Vermont, were spotted one day "drinking, or pretending to drink" from beer bottles discarded the night before by teenagers who'd been drinking at the playground of Neshobe Elementary School. To nip this obvious alcoholism in the bud, the principal of the school ordered all sixty-four of the school's sixth graders to be given Breathalyzer tests. The story failed to reveal if any guilty parties were tossed into the drunk tank.

THE DUMBEST BANK ROBBER OF 1987

A man in Orlando, Florida, handed a bank teller a note that read, "Give me all your money or else I'll shoot you. Bang!" The teller gave the man some money and he fled. He was picked up a couple of hours later, however—he'd written the note on the back of his parole card.

ON THE EQUAL RIGHTS FRONT...

Catherine Pollard, a sixty-nine-year-old Connecticut woman, lost her appeal in the Connecticut Supreme Court, after a thirteen-year legal battle to become the nation's first female Boy Scout leader. Seems the Boy Scouts thought that all sorts of terrible things would happen to American youth if sissy females were allowed to teach them how to tie knots, etc.

NEWS OF THE BABY BELLS

Wonder how the phone company spends your money? So do state regulators in California, who are trying to find a reason why **Pacific Bell** spent a whopping $30 million on secret employee brainwashing sessions based on the teachings of a very odd Russian mystic, George Gurdjieff.

Considering our huge trade deficit with Japan, Wisconsin Senator **Robert W. Kasten, Jr.,** was appalled to discover that the Senate gift shop sold souvenir postcards printed in Japan. Commented the senator, "My favorite card was the one showing the Iwo Jima monument. We thought we knew which side won that battle. But now we know who's really winning."

FOR THE TRULY GULLIBLE . . .

Former TV evangelist **Rex Humbard** mailed 122,000 brown paper "resurrection prayer rugs" to people on his mailing list. He suggested that the rugs could produce health, prosperity, and miracles—if the recipients proved their faith by sending $10 back to him.

A Michigan state official announced that the black bear will symbolize the 150th anniversary of the Wolverine State—because there's no proof that a single wolverine ever lived in the entire state.

THE WORLD'S DUMBEST WAR

The Iran-Iraq War has resulted in an estimated 1 million deaths over the last six years—with no appreciable advantage to either side.

SHIRT SUIT

A sex discrimination suit was filed against the Vistacion Valley Laundry in San Francisco, because the laundry charges nearly twice as much to clean a woman's shirt as it does to clean a man's shirt. The laundry replied that it needs more money to do women's shirts because they button on the left rather than the right. Huh?

THE MOST ABSURD TESTIMONY OF THE YEAR

The issue of the qualifications of **Mary Beth Whitehead,** surrogate mother of "Baby M," was a serious matter. One can only hope that the judge's decision

BOY, IS THAT DUMB!

ignored the testimony of an eminent psychiatrist, who said Whitehead was an awkward mother, partly because she didn't play patty-cake properly.

The testimony shocked tens of millions of parents, who assumed that even six-month-old babies knew how to play the game. No word on whether the shrink is franchising a nationwide "teach your baby patty-cake" school.

PASSION FLOWER SLIGHTLY WILTED

Romina Danielson, the twenty-three-year-old woman who claims she was Peter Holm's "passion flower," has been busily trying to use the notoriety caused by her appearance at the **Joan Collins–Peter Holm** divorce trial to make herself a celebrity. She's been announcing her arrival at restaurants as a media event, then giving press conferences to hand out photographs and proclaim that someday she would be the "biggest star." One slight hitch in her projected career: She bragged to reporters that she'd posed nude for *Playboy* test photos. According to a *Playboy* spokesman, however, the magazine has no further interest in her. The spokesman reportedly commented, "Not everyone has what it takes."

GREAT MOMENTS IN ACADEMIC RESEARCH

Fortune magazine reported a five-year academic study, entitled "Tears and Weeping among Professional

Women," that discovered women cry more frequently than men at the office. In a report that classifies as one of the major non-surprises of the year, the academics who conducted the study claimed that the average cry lasts six minutes.

DID HE TAKE THE HYPOCRITE'S OATH?

At Beebe Hospital in Lewes, Delaware, Dr. Robert Spicer refused to operate on a man who had a deep cut in his foot. The doctor's reason: The man looked gay, and the noble physician feared that he might have AIDS. So he had the guy flown by helicopter to a hospital in Washington, D.C. Turns out the guy didn't need surgery and didn't have AIDS.

DUMBEST CAR THEFT

The red and white Jeep parked on a Charleston, West Virginia, street had not only been featured in thousands of campaign ads but also was plastered with campaign stickers carrying the name of its owner, West Virginia Secretary of State **Ken Hechler**. Despite that, a thirty-seven-year-old man stole the Jeep.

Naturally, he was picked up less than ten minutes after the police were notified that the Jeep had been stolen. Commented the owner, "I imagine this person will be a candidate for the illiteracy program."

DUMB, DUMB, DUMB, DUMB . . .

For some bizarre reason, nineteen-year-old Sean Sanders developed a dangerous habit—breaking into Pittsburgh police headquarters to burglarize the place. In six separate break-ins, he took computers, calculators, petty cash, even cookies. And he got away clean—or so he thought.

It seems Sanders, on one of his forays, discovered a Polaroid camera and couldn't resist taking his own picture. Evidently not realizing that the picture took time to develop, he tossed what appeared to be a blank negative in the trash.

Sure enough, cops found the "picture-perfect" evidence, completely developed. An officer later spotted Sanders walking in downtown Pittsburgh and hauled him in. The Polaroid was in his gym bag.

By the way, Sanders made yet another dumb mistake: When he was arrested, police were in the process of tracing two library books he'd left at police headquarters.

STUPIDITY IN THE COLA WARS

A Coca-Cola worker reached an out-of-court settlement in a suit alleging that she was fired from her job because she was engaged to an employee of Pepsi-Cola. Amanda Blake Conklin charged that the Coca-Cola Bottling Company of Northampton, Massachusetts told her she either had to break her engagement, persuade her fiancé to quit his job, or quit her own job. She was fired when she failed to follow the ultimatum.

IF YOU BELIEVE THIS...

Joan Collins, emerging from court hearings related to her divorce action against fourth husband **Peter Holm**, shouted: "I'll never, ever marry again. No way!"

THE EGG ON THE FACE AWARD, ENTERTAINMENT DIVISION

Goes to actor-singer **Kris Kristofferson**. Kristofferson sang at a benefit in Albany, New York, then was presented with an expensive plaque. After the performance, theater employees found the plaque in a pile of trash outside the theater. A spokesman for Kristofferson hurriedly explained that "Basically, it ended up in the garbage by mistake."

THE IF-YOU-BELIEVE-THIS SCAM OF THE YEAR

The postcard reads, "Congratulations, you have won a glamorous, fun-filled vacation in Florida." In 1987, over

1 million Americans fell for phony travel scams after receiving postcards or telephone calls of this kind from over a hundred different companies in Florida, Texas, and California.

ALL THE NEWS YOU CAN'T BELIEVE

The prestigious *New York Times Magazine* got stung a couple times in 1987. In June, the magazine ran a first-person story written by a woman who was supposedly a humble secretary in New Jersey who slaved away nights to write a best-selling novel. It turns out the "secretary" was a Harvard-educated woman who was a former editor at a major publishing house.

A few weeks later, the magazine ran a large picture of a drug bust—which turned out to be a staged photograph taken four years previously for an advertisement.

THE FATHER, SON, AND HOLY SMOKE

Harvard Divinity School student Erwin Rupert filed suit against the Cambridge, Massachusetts, no-smoking law, saying it restricted his right to freedom of religion. Rupert is a member of the Society of the Peace Pipe, which recognizes tobacco as a deity, and whose members worship through smoking together. Rupert commented, "Tobacco is more than wine or bread, it's a deity, an embodiment of God." And you thought cigars were just smelly!

MORE TAX DOLLARS AT WORK

Ex-Maryland Governor **Harry Hughes** used $6,000 in state money to have his wife's clothes altered. The IRS went after him for taxes on the money, claiming it wasn't a legitimate business expense.

THE 1987 AWARD FOR ACHIEVEMENT IN FICTION

Goes to a U.S. Justice Department attorney who was caught naked in bed with a naked hooker when Washington, D.C., police raided a brothel. The attorney testified to a grand jury that "he had never been to the premises before and he had not engaged in any sexual conduct on the evening in question." Guess the rest of us must just have dirty minds, to see anything sexual about lying naked in bed with a naked hooker.

P.S., the attorney later changed his story to avoid going to jail.

IN THE THRILL-OF-A-LIFETIME DEPARTMENT...

It may even be worth a trip to Seattle. Certainly residents of that Washington city have been pouring into the Uptown Expresso juice bar and forking over their quarters. And what's the attraction? On display in the bar is a magenta polyester gown worn by **Vanna White** on *Wheel of Fortune*. And for just 25 cents, you thrill-seekers can actually touch the cloth that touched Vanna. Wow!

WHITE ELEPHANT OF THE YEAR

The unfinished new U.S. embassy building in Moscow is reportedly so riddled with electronic listening devices embedded in the walls that it may have to be demolished. Other uses for the building have been suggested, but there's no truth to the rumor that it will be shipped to the United States and used as a monastery for American presidential candidates.

ADDICTED TO LOTTO

David and Patricia Libby of Hamden, Connecticut, decided to move to North Carolina for a novel reason; it has no state-sponsored gambling. It seems that David had an odd gambling addiction—he couldn't stop buying state lottery tickets. The compulsion, which lasted ten years and cost him his first marriage, peaked when he bought a whopping $12,000 worth of Connecticut state lottery tickets. Unable to conquer his urge to hang around lottery terminals, Libby decided to go away from temptation.

IN THE PICTURES-WE-DIDN'T-SEE DEPARTMENT

Austin Miles, a circus ringmaster turned preacher, told the *Washington Post* that he saw "Jim [Bakker] frolicking in the nude with three other men in a steam room. They were dancing around and taking turns lying on a table, massaging each other."

Another man, a vice president of PTL, **Jim Bakker**'s organization, also charged that the evangelist made a homosexual pass at him in Bakker's bedroom.

No photographic evidence exists of the incidents, and Bakker has denied the charges.

SLIP OF THE TONGUE

An aide for Governor Hunt of Alabama dismissed his boss's remarks as "just something people say" after the governor told an audience that "he never tried to Jew" a farmer that he bought peaches from.

TM MOVEMENT MOMENTARILY GROUNDED

A federal jury awarded $138,000 to a man who contended that two Transcendental Meditation organizations falsely promised that he would learn to fly. After hearing testimony about TM followers reading books with their eyes closed and flying, through a technique known as self-levitation, the jury chose to believe the man, who charged that all he learned was how to "hop with the legs folded." Ordered to pay the damages were the World Plan Executive Council–United States and the Maharishi International University of Fairfield, Iowa.

CASH FOR THE REBORN

After evangelist **Oral Roberts** publicly claimed to have brought many people back from the dead, the publisher of three tabloids—the *Globe*, the *National Examiner*, and the *Sun*—placed ads offering cash rewards for the story of anyone who was actually reborn. The tabloids to date haven't paid a cent.

IS SOMETHING FISHY IN KEY WEST?

Evidently, being mayor of Key West, Florida, is the luckiest job in the world. In 1987, Mayor Tom Sawyer won a brand-new Pontiac when his ticket was drawn in the annual city raffle. In 1986, former mayor Richard Heyman won the $10,000 first prize. In 1985, then mayorial candidate Sawyer was the winner of a gold bar valued at $10,000. Wonder how many tickets they're going to sell to non-mayors in 1988?

WE'VE HEARD OF FAMILY PLANNING, BUT...

For the second time, two sisters in Mesa, Arizona, gave birth to babies on the same day at the same hospital with the same doctor within an hour of each other. No, they're not twins—and they don't share the same husband.

YOU TALK ABOUT BAD FOR BUSINESS...

A male prostitute, who'd been arrested sixty-six times for conducting his business, was ordered by the Mississippi Health Department not to have sex with a "date" without first telling the man that he's a carrier of the AIDS virus. Said a state official, "Having the virus is no crime. Giving it to somebody else knowingly ought to be."

Do state officials really believe the guy is going to start his solicitation by saying, "Hey, there, big guy, wanta have some fun with a guy who's got AIDS?"

NURSES BARE ALL

Officials at Holy Cross Hospital in Silver Spring, Maryland, said a camera secretly installed in the nurses' room was meant to catch a nurse suspected of stealing drugs—but the camera transmitted pictures that played on the TV set in the doctors' lounge.

AND EXACTLY WHO MAY THAT BE?

A furrier whose company is selling the Liberace Concerto Collection, commented, "We will be very particular with who buys them [$10,000 fur coats fashioned to look like pianos], because we don't want anyone wearing them who **Liberace** wouldn't have felt comfortable with."

AND WHAT DID THE DEAD GUY HAVE TO SAY?

Shirley MacLaine, at the Rudolph Valentino awards ceremony, told the audience, "I was just speaking to Rudy the other night."

OBVIOUSLY

Huey Lewis remarked, "Of course it's not hip to be square."

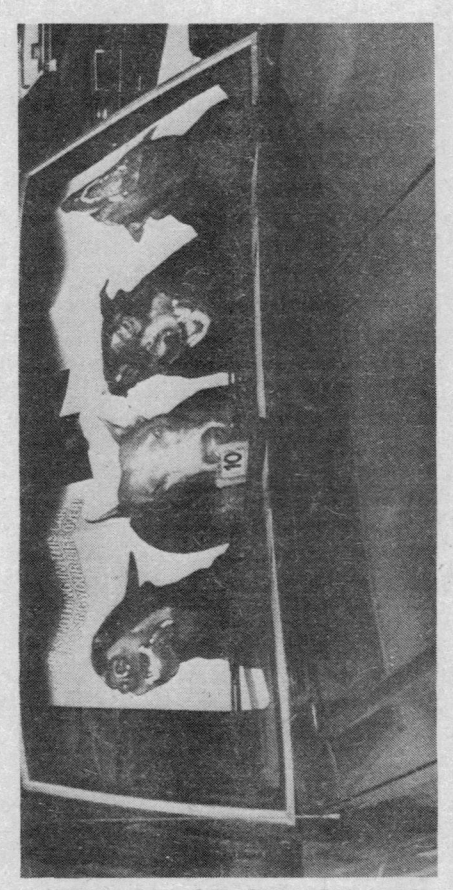

BEWARE OF SUNSHADE

Winchester, Virginia, August 28

A motorist uses a sunshade with pit bull terriers on it to ward off damages caused by the sun and would-be vandals during the dog days of summer. (Scott Mason)

9.
THE TRULY BIZARRE SCANDALS OF 1987

WHEN IT COMES TO SCANDALS, the old saying holds true: Truth is stranger than fiction. In 1987, we found ample evidence that human beings are capable of the kind of bizarre behavior normally seen only in the movies.

One story began when an employee of one of those "we rent everything" firms noticed some bloodstains on a chain saw that a customer had returned. It was hard to believe the customer was anything but a reputable citizen; he was a fifty-seven-year-old professor of political science at California State University at Fresno, a scholar who held a doctorate from New York University. But the employee called the police anyway.

What they found in the professor's apartment shocked even the hardened cops. First, they found "ample evidence" that a teenager had been murdered in the apartment, then dismembered with the chain saw. Second, they uncovered "one of the largest collections of homosexual pornography ever discovered." Finally, they saw that the professor was in the process of building a soundproof room in the middle of his living room, apparently for the purpose of committing additional bizarre murders.

Another horrible discovery was made in Philadelphia

when janitors broke into an abandoned apartment. Inside, they found the mummified body of a three-year-old girl dressed in a blue nightgown and kneeling against a bed as if in prayer.

Investigation revealed that the girl had last been seen about Christmastime, months before, and she may have starved to death. Said a cop, "All the skin was very hard from being in a warm, dry place for a period of time." The girl's mother was charged with abuse of a corpse, for not reporting the death, and an investigation was launched to see if further charges were warranted.

Not all of our bizarre stories, however, have to do with death. You'll find some amusement along with a few chills in the following pages.

SUPERSTAR SICKIE OF THE YEAR

Superstar singer **Michael Jackson** upped his offer to the London Hospital Medical College to a whopping $1 million. What does he want in return for the money? Jackson is determined to obtain the skeletal remains of the grotesquely deformed **John Merrick**, the Elephant Man. Spokesmen for the singer stated that he wants the remains for his private museum of "curiosities."

SICK, SICK, SICK

Edward Fisch, thrity-eight, of Putnam Valley, New York was arrested by police and charged with mixing

THIS IS NOT A DRIVE-THRU!

Cherry Hill, New Jersey, March 20

Clerk Karl Pearce peers over the counter at a car which slammed through the window of this 7-11. The gas pedal allegedly stuck, causing the car to accelerate into the store. (Jim Bonner) drain cleaner in with the baby food fed to his eight-month-old daughter.

THE SICKEST CRIME OF THE YEAR

A woman in Albuquerque, New Mexico, was taken into custody and charged with kidnapping a pregnant woman, strangling her, then stealing the baby from her womb by a "crude Caesarean operation." The woman allegedly lurked outside a clinic at Kirtland Air Force Base waiting for any pregnant woman who was near term to emerge. After the crime, the alleged murderer turned up at the hospital with the baby, claiming it was hers.

OUR CREATIVE AD OF THE YEAR AWARD...

Goes to tire store owner Sam Behr, who bought time on television to announce that "I just got a message from upstairs. It says I gotta sell 80,000 tires in the next month or I'm gonna die." Admirers of TV evangelist **Oral Roberts**, whom Behr was spoofing, temporarily got stations to pull the commercial, but eventually it was back on the air. No word, though, on how many cars Behr claims to have brought back from the dead.

WOULD THE BABY CALL HER MAMA GRANDMA?

Ever hear the old joke about the woman who had her tubes tied because she didn't want any more grandchildren? Someone should have told it to forty-eight-year-old Pat Anthony of South Africa, who's pregnant with not one, but three grandchildren. Yes, it's true—Anthony was implanted with the embryos of triplets from her daughter, who can't have any more children.

WASP DOWNS PLANE

A passenger in a single-engine plane took a swat at a wasp shortly after takeoff from the Orlando, Florida, airport. But instead of the insect, he hit the controls, sending the plane into a nosedive. The propeller of the plane hit the ground before the pilot regained control, causing $50,000 in damage. The passenger was unhurt in the crash, but his duel with the wasp came out a draw: He was stung and the wasp died.

NOW, IF YOU CAN ADD A LITTLE BUMP AND GRIND...

A Daytona Beach, Florida, woman who was suing the Lovable Company was ordered by Florida's Fifth District Court of Appeal to expose her breasts to the company's attorneys for exactly two minutes. The woman claimed that dye in the company's bra had turned her breasts permanently black. The thirty-five-year-old woman protested, "It's inhumane to expect me to expose myself to strangers." The Lovable lawyer denied any attempt to embarrass the woman, claiming that it would be impossible for the company to decide whether to pay damages unless they saw the actual damage.

HE'S GOING TO THE DOGS

Britain's **Lord Avebury**, a member of the House of Lords, changed his will to direct that after his death, his body be cut up and fed to stray dogs in south London. His Lordship, who recently converted to Buddhism, made the request because he believed that everything, including himself, should be recycled.

The dogs, however, may not get a chance to dine on a peer. The manager of a home for stray dogs said, "As a veterinary surgeon I am sure there's a lot of nutritional value in the noble lord, and the dogs are not fussy. But we just couldn't do it."

Twenty tearful relatives and friends attended funeral services for Captain A. G. Maximillian Cricket at the First Presbyterian Church in Santa Clara, California.

Sound like a strange name? That's because Max wasn't a person; he was a parrot. The cause of the tragedy—Max was smashed by a car door.

HUMANE EXECUTIVE OF THE YEAR

In Martinsville, Virginia, Bassett Furniture Industries executive Michael D. DeHart, thirty-four, was convicted of cruelty to animals after he ordered a plant worker to toss five kittens into a boiler furnace. What does Bassett manufacture, you ask? Among other things, baby furniture.

THE WORST TEENAGE FAD

Four teenagers in California died last year as a result of the newest drug fad—sniffing typewriter correction fluid. The biggest users are twelve- to fourteen-year-olds, who pay about $1.49 for a bottle. The fluid has low concentrations of chemicals linked to heart failure and convulsions.

IS GOD A CELESTIAL MOBSTER?

Two aerospace engineers filed a lawsuit against evangelist **Oral Roberts**, accusing him of raising $8.7 million dollars by falsely portraying God as a blackmailer. In January 1987, the evangelist announced that God had told him he had to raise $8 million for medical missionary scholarships or God would "call him home." The lawsuit asked that Roberts be required to notify donors that they could get their money back.

WHY DON'T YOU ASK LEN BIAS, COACH?

The most bizarre sports statement of the year came from former University of Maryland basketball head coach **Lefty Driesell**, who resigned from his job after star player **Len Bias** had died of a cocaine overdose. Driesell later told a conference on drugs in sports: "I'm a firm believer that if you know how to use cocaine and use it properly, it can make you play better." Driesell reached his interesting conclusion while writing a 1957 master's thesis based on research done in 1941.

MOST BIZARRE KIDNAPPING OF 1987

Thieves broke into the Buenos Aires tomb of former Argentine President **Juan Perón**, opened the coffin, and cut off the ex-dictator's hands. They then demanded some fancy digits of their own for the return of the hands—a ransom of $8 million.

THE WORST NEW LAW OF 1987

The city of Millbrae, California, passed a law providing penalties of six months in jail and a $500 fine for motorized wheelchairs caught traveling more than 3 miles per hour—which is slower than the average pedestrian walks. Said one of the outraged spokespeople for the disabled: "It's difficult enough for the disabled as it is, without someone clocking their wheelchairs with a radar gun."

REAGAN'S SON ABUSED

In a 1987 biography, **Michael Reagan**, adopted son of **Ronald Reagan** and ex-wife **Jane Wyman**, revealed that he was sexually abused by a camp counselor at age seven. Until last year, he never told his father. The younger Reagan also revealed that after his parents' divorce, he felt abandoned by both of them; until age ten, he thought his mother was a black cook named Carrie.

FRONT PAGE STORY

In the small town of Hornell, New York, rumors about Debra French raged like a prairie fire. Miss French, who described herself as "a normal, healthy, unattached twenty-eight-year-old woman" who liked to frequent taverns and go out with different men, found that her mother was receiving condolences from friends who thought Debra had died of AIDS. The rumor that she had the disease spread unchecked, from Snoopy's Bar to the health club where Debra worked out. When the health club manager urged Debra to take an AIDS test because other members were afraid of getting her disease, she knew it had gone too far. She took the test, then had her doctor write a letter to the Hornell *Evening Tribune* verifying that the test was negative. The rumor was such big news that the negative test results produced a front page story.

OVERREACTION, VOLUME ONE

Northwest Airline announced that its policy is to refuse to fly passengers with AIDS. Since AIDS is transmitted only through intimate contact, we're decidedly curious about what goes on when Northwest planes are aloft.

THE MOST BIZARRE STORY OF 1987

Dr. J. Brendan Wynne of the Osteopathic Medical Center in Philadelphia wrote a letter to the American Medical Association warning physicians of the dangers of vacuum toilets on airplanes and ships. Dr. Wynne told the AMA he was summoned to the assistance of a fellow passenger on a cruise ship, who had "several feet of small intestine" sucked out of her after flushing the toilet.

※

Fourteen current and former inmates of the Woodbury County Jail in Sioux City, Iowa, filed a lawsuit claiming that officials of the jail tried to murder them. The alleged weapon: a communal razor which the inmates were forced to use, supposedly exposing them to the risk of catching AIDS.

※

AIDS PHOBIA

A Brooklyn, New York, woman filed suit against her husband, seeking damages for "intentional infliction of emotional distress." The charge: He revealed to a marriage counselor that he'd had many homosexual encounters. Knowledge of her husband's gay sex life allegedly gave the woman a phobia that she had AIDS—even though her husband's blood tests for AIDS were negative. So she's suing because she's petrified of having a disease she can't possibly have. Huh?

※

A Denton, Texas, man shot and killed his nephew, whom he had accused of infecting him with AIDS by biting him. AIDS tests were negative.

HUSBAND AND FATHER OF THE YEAR AWARD

Goes to Joseph Austin, twenty-two, of Allegan, Michigan, who was convicted of wrapping his naked wife and seven-year-old stepdaughter in duct tape, then trying to sell them as slaves for $150.

WHEN E. F. HUTTON TALKS, MORONS LISTEN

E. F. Hutton and Company, buffeted by scandal, decided to educate their employees about sound business practices by issuing *The Hutton Coloring Book*. The company decided on a coloring book so the message would be clear. Question: Would you invest with brokers who had to be talked to like this?

> "We're no longer the nicest house on the block. . . . If we don't fix our problem soon, someone could even take our house away."

MOTHER OF THE YEAR

From an interview with **Jacqueline Stallone, Sylvester Stallone's** mother, as reported in *Us* magazine:

- Her advice to her teenage son about dating: "I told him to get all the sex he could before he got married, but not to get girls pregnant."
- Future marital advice for her son: "He should have a nice big house in the country with ten children all looking like him. Then he can take total charge. . . . This would be his island, his first love. He should have a mistress of every nationality. He should have a Miss Italy, Miss Sweden here, Miss Denmark there. This way he is taking care of the whole world."
- Her one wish for her son: "That he have ten children and no wives."

WEIRDEST FETISH OF THE YEAR

Jimmy Allen Terrell, thirty-four, was arrested in Oklahoma City for posing as a doctor. It seems Terrell called twenty to thirty women listed in newspaper birth announcements. He allegedly told them the city hospital needed donations of breast milk for premature babies, then talked two women into letting him drain their breasts.

ARMS DEALER GETS EARS

In one of those fascinating sidelights of the news, *Time* magazine reported that Sarkis Soghanalian, a

300-pound Turkish-born Lebanese citizen living in Miami, was an arms dealer who specialized in selling helicopters to Iraq, and reportedly received gifts of "jars of severed human ears from clients."

MOST BIZARRE CHARITY REQUEST OF THE YEAR

Fortune magazine reported that a very prominent businessman received the following mailing from the International Youth Development Organization, Inc.:

> You have been selected as a contributor to our Plates of the Great collection. We request you send us a Plate you have eaten off and a cover letter stating so. . . . This is a way of helping young and old alike realize that a great person who has many achievements to their favor are human and eat the same as a poor person wondering if they will ever amount to a thing. . . . Your plate will be exhibited along with other great folk like Henry Ford, Greer Garson . . . and many others.

MOST UNUSUAL SENTENCE OF THE YEAR

After a Butler (Indiana) University student was found guilty of fighting on campus, the judge gave him a choice—either make the football team or go to jail.

TALK ABOUT WEDDING PRIDE

Linda Pritchard wore a safari suit instead of a white gown at her wedding. Her choice had nothing to do with any prejudice against the ritual white: she wore the safari suit because white might have riled the six lions that were invited to the ceremony.

Pritchard married fellow lion tamer Julius Von Uhl—in a 32-foot cage with the lions they train in a circus.

ANOTHER ENTRY IN THE BIZARRE CHARITY DEPARTMENT

The two Miami *Herald* reporters who staked out **Gary Hart's** Washington town house and discovered the presence there of **Donna Rice** donated the shoes they wore to be auctioned off for the benefit of a journalism program for minority students.

YOU THINK YOU'VE GOT PROBLEMS WITH THE NEIGHBORS

More than a thousand visitors a week have been strolling by Arlene Gardner's house in Nashville, Tennessee. The attraction: When Gardner's neighbor

Katherine Partin flips on her front porch light, Gardner believes the face of Jesus is reflected on her freezer. Gardner says, "It's the work of God. I was told that in a dream. Praise the Lord, it's the work of God."

Some visitors claim to see Jesus, some see nothing, and others claim the reflection looks more like Willie Nelson. One skeptic commented, "When the good Lord comes, he won't come on a major appliance."

YOU CAN'T LET THE LITTLE THINGS BOTHER YOU

Scott Walker, twenty-two, of Fort Lauderdale, Florida, evidently believes that you can't let little things damage your marriage. That's why he didn't get mad when his wife tried to hire a hit man to kill him.

According to police, Sonya Walker, nineteen, answered a personal ad placed by a businessman seeking a young woman. She wrote him that she'd love to meet him, only she needed to become a widow first. The letter found its way to police, who had an undercover agent meet with Mrs. Walker. She asked the undercover agent to break into her apartment, shoot her husband, and dump his body into the Everglades in exchange for $5,000. She wrote a check for $100 as a down payment.

Mr. Walker, however, stands by his wife, who told him after her arrest that she just got "confused." He hired a lawyer for her. His final comment: "Like any marriage, ours had its high points and low points."

THANKS FOR THE MAMMARIES

A Nashville, Tennessee, woman realized her lifetime dream when she won a radio station giveaway. Her prize: free breast enlargement surgery. Patty Chunn, twenty-six, was so ecstatic that she sang a song for station workers, to the tune of "Oh, Lord, It's Hard to Be Humble." In part, the song went like this:

Oh, Lord, it's hard to be happy
When your chest is as flat as a wall;
I can't even wear those cute tube tops,
'Cause I'm always afraid that they'll fall.

The woman reported that her husband "was as excited as I am."

BEATING THE BOOZE RIGHT OUT OF THEM

Alcohol-abuse therapist Alfred J. O'Conner had a novel approach to treating alcoholics—and it landed him in court. To get the drunks off the bottle, he'd order them to strip naked; then he would flog them. In a plea bargain arrangement, he pleaded guilty to fourth-degree criminal sexual conduct.

Margaret Kelly Michaels, twenty-five, was charged with 163 counts of sexually abusing, assaulting, and molesting thirty-one children in her class at the Wee Care Day Nursery in Maplewood, New Jersey. The prosecutor charged that Michaels played the piano in the nude, made both boys and girls strip to perform sex acts with her, and used knives and spoons to molest them.

MURDER BY BLOOD

Los Angeles County prosecutors charged twenty-nine-year-old Joseph Edward Markowski with attempted murder—for selling his blood when he knew he was infected with the AIDS virus. Markowski allegedly had two very dangerous ways of earning a living—he gave blood twenty-three times, and he "turned tricks" as a male prostitute—another way to pass along the deadly virus.

WHERE WAS ESPN?

Is it the new sport of the 1980s? Maybe not, but it certainly excites the folks in Ticonderoga, New York, who conduct it as an annual fund-raiser for the town's fireworks display. The sport: cow-drop bingo.

Here are the rules: Divide a large field into 289

squares; sell the squares for $5 each; then let a cow loose in the field and wait to see which square the cow fertilizes first. According to observers, spectators screamed and howled for thirty minutes while the cow decided whom to honor. If that isn't excitement, we don't know what is.

BABY MURDER

A twenty-two-year-old San Francisco woman was arrested in Florida and extradited to Kansas City, Missouri. The charges: She gave birth to a baby in an airplane bathroom during a stopover in Kansas City, killed the baby, then dumped the body in a bathroom trash bin at the Miami, Florida, airport.

THE BABY MACHINE

The controversy began when Washington, D.C., Mayor **Marion Barry, Jr.,** was touring an emergency city shelter for homeless families. He was confronted by thirty-five-year-old Jacqueline Williams, who lived at the shelter with her second husband and her fourteen children. Williams demanded to know why the mayor wasn't "doing his job" and getting her a better place to live. The mayor who, like Williams, is black, replied that he wanted to know why the woman didn't stop having children. He pointed out that the city was already spending an incredible $120,000 a year to feed and house Williams's family.

Later, Mayor Barry used Williams as an example of the development of a "permanent underclass" of people who were having more and more babies so as to get more and more government assistance. In reply, Williams said that she was going to keep having children "until God stops me." She also said she'd been almost continuously pregnant since age sixteen, and she added, "I don't want to mess my body up with birth control." Oh, yes—she was pregnant with her fifteenth child at the time.

ORAL ROBERTS MUGGED

Evangelist **Oral Roberts** claimed he was mugged—and the culprit was that old devil, the devil himself. Said Roberts, "The devil came to my room just a few nights ago, and I felt those hands on my throat and he was choking the life out of me. I yelled to my wife, 'Honey, come!'"

Fortunately, Mrs. Roberts must be a calm and experienced exorcist. She "rebuked" the naughty demon and "commanded the devil to get out of my room." No word if Roberts filed a police complaint.

PARENTS NEED EDUCATION

Parents of students in Leesville, Louisiana, are at least as badly in need of classroom instruction as the students. Assistant high school principal Richard Carter presented to the school board several samples of excuse notes written by parents to the school. Among them were the following:

- My son is under the doctor's care and should not take P.E. today. Please execute him.
- Please excuse Mary for being absent. She was sick and I had her shot.
- Please ackuse Fred of being absent on Jan. 28, 29, 30, 31, 32, and 33.
- Mary was absent from school yesterday as she was having a gangover.
- Please excuse Mary from Jim yesterday. She is administrating.
- Please excuse Fred for being absent. He had a cold and could not breed well.
- Please excuse Mary. She has been sick and under the doctor.
- Please excuse Fred for being. It was his father's fault.
- Please scuse Mary from being absent yesterday. She was in bed with gramps.
- Please excuse Fred from P.E. for a few days. He fell yesterday out of a tree and misplaced his hip.
- Mary could not come to school today because she was bothered by very close veins.
- Fred has an acre in his side.

TALK ABOUT BAD DAYS...

Randy Hill, fifty-five, kept a vigil by his wife's bedside at St. Joseph's Hospital in Syracuse, New York, after doctors told him she was near death. But he grew increasingly worried that he'd been unable to contact his twenty-eight-year-old daughter for two days. So he rushed to her apartment—and found her lying on the floor dead, having been strangled with the belt of her bath robe. After he called police, he raced back to be with his wife, who died nine hours later.

PRISONERS GOT A BANG OUT OF THE GAME

Things must have really been slow on the job for prison guard Steven McGill. He allegedly recruited some inmates for a game of Russian roulette—with real bullets in his gun. The game abruptly ended when one inmate fatally shot himself in the head. McGill was sentenced to twelve years as an inmate for depriving the con of his civil rights.

MOST BIZARRE EXAMPLE OF RACIAL DISCRIMINATION IN 1987

A federal lawsuit was filed in Portsmouth, Virginia, against three nightclubs that featured nude dancing. The charge: The clubs charged blacks a $6 cover to watch the naked women, while whites were admitted for $2.

THE CONDOM CLERIC

The Reverend **Carl Thitchener**, pastor of the Unitarian Universalist Church of Amherst, New York, a suburb of Buffalo, made national headlines when he passed out condoms to his congregation during a sermon on AIDS.

A few days later, he made headlines again—this time with his arrest record. It seems that Thitchener was first arrested in 1958 for standing in a Rochester, New York, backyard and flashing passersby "with his trousers and shorts off." In 1982, two years after he was ordained, he was picked up "wearing little or no clothing" outside a church where a troop of Brownie scouts was meeting; he pleaded guilty to disorderly conduct. In 1984, the condom cleric was arrested for driving while intoxicated.

JUST PLAIN SICK

Everett Mortensen, sixty-seven, of San Jose, California, was charged with murder. His alleged crime: allowing his invalid eighty-five-year-old mother to lie helpless on the floor for seven days after she fell out of her wheelchair. The mother died in a hospital the day after paramedics, summoned by a neighbor, rescued her.

10.
EVERY DAY, IN AMERICA . . .

YOU MAY NOT REALIZE IT, but all sorts of sin and trouble swirl around you every single day. As you go about your daily business, your countrymen are handing out about $42.3 million to prostitutes. Including postmen, about 12,000 unlucky people are bitten by dogs, while about the same number of students are beaten up by other kids at school.

While all this is going on, some of your neighbors are scheming to steal $34 million a day from their employers, and others are busy writing about a million bad checks. Some of that money goes toward the $10 million or so a day people spend on pornography.

All the while, the federal government is spending $2.6 billion of your dollars and going $556 million deeper in debt. In the process, the government wastes an estimated $75 million a day.

What's going on with your kids? Some 14,000 of them are dropping out of school; 5,000 are being arrested; 1.4 million are smoking marijuana; and nearly 3 million are having a drink.

All the while you're getting older. About 6,400 of you are turning fifty, and about 6,000 are turning sixty-five.

Interested in finding out more about what your fellow Americans are doing today? Read on.

EVERY DAY IN AMERICA . . .

- 2,105 babies are born out of wedlock, 738 to teenage mothers.
- 308 babies are born with major birth defects.
- 4,150 abortions are performed.
- 700,000 high school seniors attend classes, even though they can't read.
- Television minister **Jimmy Swaggart** rakes in a cool $500,000 in daily donations.
- 685 emergency patients are turned away from hospitals without treatment because they don't have medical insurance.
- Organized crime rakes in $249,315,068.
- 225 buildings are torched by arsonists.
- 5 public officials are indicted or convicted.
- 590 sixteen-year-old girls lose their virginity.
- 58 people develop AIDS; 21,000,000 Americans have sex but don't develop AIDS.
- 30,137 people get a sexually transmitted disease other than AIDS.
- 95,616 property and violent crimes are committed.
- 15,694 homes are burglarized.
- 11,902 people are assaulted.
- 2,735 people are robbed.
- 421 women are raped.
- Guilt-ridden citizens anonymously send $1,044 to the U.S. government's "conscience" fund.
- Street criminals rip off victims for $10,958,904.
- White-collar criminals steal $109,589,041.
- 14 homosexuals are assaulted by "gay-bashers"—over twice as many as were attacked daily the year before, an increase attributed to hysteria over AIDS.
- "The Great Satan"—otherwise known as the United States—imports $1,558,904 in products from Iran.
- $843,835,616 is spent to educate American young people, 20 percent of whom won't be able to read at more than a fifth grade level when they finish school.
- Americans lose $24,657,534 in fire damage.
- American teenagers spend $191,780,082, half of which comes from their parents.

WHERE THERE'S SMOKE, THERE'S IRE

Hastings, Michigan, August 25

Flora Mae, 79, and Lyle Biddle, 82, hoist one of more than 5,000 marijuana plants they discovered growing on or near their property in Barry County. Sheriff's officials say that since last week, the couple eliminated plants estimated to be worth $3 million.

EVERY DAY IN AMERICA ...

- The average New York City streetwalker earns $1,500.
- 959 Americans die from cigarette smoking.
- 1,400 unmarried couples move in together.
- 3,164 couples get divorced.
- 4,367 people remarry.
- 5,205 children age ten to seventeen are arrested.
- 5,500 children run away from home.
- 4,032 children under age six are treated for poisoning.
- Children thirteen and under watch 192 million hours of television.
- The average mother spends eleven minutes of quality time with her children; the average father spends eight minutes.
- 23,148 drivers get speeding tickets.
- 2,240 cars are stolen.
- 51,507 motor vehicle accidents take place.
- 13,813 people are injured in motor vehicle accidents.
- 118 people are killed in motor vehicle accidents.
- 5 people are accidently killed by guns.
- 57,500,000 Americans skip breakfast.
- Americans wager $484 million—fifteen times what they contribute to churches.
- 2,493 Americans are diagnosed as having cancer.
- 82 people kill themselves; of these, 48 shoot themselves; 17 take drugs or poison, 11 hang themselves.
- 2,897,000 adults are sick in bed.
- 101,369 people are hospitalized.
- 49,315 people have plastic surgery.
- American adults consume 1.4 billion calories more than they need, thus gaining 400,000 pounds.
- About 16 million men and 11 million women have at least one alcoholic drink.
- 64,208 households are touched by crime.
- 713,000 people are in jail.
- 22 people escape from jail.

EVERY DAY IN AMERICA...

- Americans charge $548 million on nearly 1 billion credit cards.
- Americans earn about $383 million in "under the table" money.
- 4,962 taxpayers are audited by the IRS.
- 822 people declare personal bankruptcy.
- Drug dealers earn $123 million.
- Americans smoke 87,000 bales of marijuana and snort 380 pounds of cocaine.
- American industry produces 15 billion pounds of hazardous waste.

11.
THE EXCLUSIVE SCANDAL ANNUAL "SIN-DEX"

AFTER ENOUGH EXPOSURE to the media—for example, after watching a couple hours of rock videos on MTV—one begins to wonder if anything is considered a sin these days. The question is an important one here at the Paragon Project, since sin and scandal are all part of the same package. We begin to realize that we'd do a lot better job collecting scandals if we had an up to date idea about what you readers consider to be the worst—and least offensive—sins.

To find the answer, we conducted a survey, our exclusive *SCANDAL ANNUAL* Sin-dex. We asked people from all walks of life, representing all regions of the United States and Canada, ranging in age from 18 to 70, to rate a number of "sins" on a scale of 10 (the worst sin) to 1 (almost inoffensive). While we don't claim our sampling is as statistically perfect as a Gallup Poll, we did find that the surveys we tallied gave a surprisingly consistant picture (with a few exceptions) of what you readers believe is immoral these days.

First, let's talk about the exceptions. For a small number of activities, we discovered almost no middle ground—our respondents either considered them a major sin or not a sin at all. Not surprisingly, the most polarity was on the issue of *abortion*: a majority of those surveyed considered it not a sin, while a minority ranked it with murder, the number one worst sin. The other issues on which we discovered two widely diverse schools of thought were: *homosexuality, having AIDS, not believing in God*, and, to a lesser extent, *living together without marriage*.

Now, on to our major findings. Our Sin-dex revealed beyond a doubt that fear of getting sexual disease, particularly AIDS, is dominating the thoughts of you readers these days. Both *lying about a sexual disease* and *lying about birth control* ranked right up near the top of our Sin-dex, while more "old-fashioned" sexual sins such as adultery and spouse-swapping were way down the list. While the opponents of pornography, permissiveness in the movies, and sex education are very vocal, our survey found that the overwhelming majority of our respondents were very tolerant of *sex education, nudity in the movies, giving condoms to teenagers*, and even *watching x-rated videos*. Our Sin-dex also revealed that most of you see very little wrong in surrogate motherhood or artificial insemination.

Another major discovery: the campaign against drunk driving has won the hearts of almost all of you. While almost everyone approves of drinking, *driving while intoxicated* was ranked as the 7th worst sin on the list. *Serving alcohol to minors* also ranked relatively high, above using drugs.

The third surprise was our respondents' very high tolerance for white collar crime, such as embezzlement, stock fraud, etc. Despite all the Wall Street scandals, our Sin-dex lists *bank robbery* as an 8.84, a minor crime like *shoplifting* as 7.43, but stealing millions of dollars in *white collar crime* as a mere 5.67. Our readers were also very tolerant of such work-related activities as *lying to your boss, cheating on your expense account*, and *lying on a resume*.

TIGHT SPOT

Mount Bernon, Wa., April 10

A four-month-old Australian Shepherd mix, Rascal, finds himself in a tight spot after trying to take a shortcut through a gate. After a few moments of wiggling, Rascal was freed and on his way.

THE EXCLUSIVE SCANDAL ANNUAL SIN-DEX

Now it's time to let you take a look at the complete *SCANDAL ANNUAL* Sin-dex. Remember, the scale ranges from 10 (the worst sins) to 1 (the least offensive):

SCANDAL ANNUAL Sin-dex

Sin	Sin-dex rating
Murder	9.94
Sexually abusing children	9.92
Incest	9.78
Rape	9.70
Lying about a sexual disease	9.68
Spouse beating	9.31
Spying for a foreign country	9.22
Driving while intoxicated	9.04
Bank robbery	8.84
Racial harrassment	8.67
Hitting children	8.66
Cheating a customer	8.41
Sexual harrassment	8.27
Lying about birth control	8.24
Selling cocaine	7.80
Shoplifting	7.43
Lying to your spouse	7.08
Lying to your children	7.04

THE EXCLUSIVE SCANDAL ANNUAL "SIN-DEX"

Parking in a handicapped zone	6.71
Lying to Congress	6.48
Suicide	6.37
Serving alcohol to minors	6.25
Adultery	6.21
Using cocaine	6.11
Selling marijuana	6.07
Cheating on an expense account	5.81
Buying a stolen television	5.80
White collar crime	5.67
Industrial spying	5.61
Spouse swapping	5.49
Lying to your boss	5.23
Leaving scene of a minor accident	5.17
Smoking marijuana	5.08
Cheating on taxes	4.92
Smoking	4.84
Homosexuality	4.79
Producing x-rated video tapes	4.64
Killing to protect your home	4.22
Abortion	4.21
Lying on a resume	4.17
Cutting into lines	4.13

THE EXCLUSIVE SCANDAL ANNUAL SIN-DEX

Taking home office supplies	3.88
Owning an illegal firearm	3.88
Premarital sex	3.67
Calling in sick when healthy	3.63
Having AIDS	3.60
Mercy killing	3.57
Watching x-rated video tapes	3.51
Giving condoms to teenagers	3.44
Swearing	3.41
Gambling	3.36
Living together without marriage	3.33
Not believing in God	3.21
Divorce	3.12
Surrogate motherhood	3.10
Artificial insemination	3.01
Sex education	2.97
Nudity in the movies	2.91
Drinking alcohol	2.90
Nude sunbathing	2.87
Masturbation	2.22

FANCIFUL MAIL BOXES

Oakhurst, California, August 17

Lundy Hill, who lives near this Sierra Nevada town, got a bit whimsical when he put a box for air mail on a post more than twice as high as his regular mail box and placed a toilet nearby for junk mail. (Carl Crawford)

AFTERWORD
*A LOOK AHEAD AT SCANDAL
IN 1988*

WILL ANY SCANDALS IN 1988 top the delicious stories of 1987, such as the infidelity of Jim Bakker and Gary Hart? We at the Paragon Project just think they might.

Our optimism stems first of all from the 1988 elections. Nothing brings out the dark side of human nature more than the lust for power. With the campaign heating up, then the conventions and general elections, we can't believe that the only casualties will be Gary Hart and Joseph Biden.

We'll also predict more juicy scandals in the world of religion. All the publicity about the P.T.L. will no doubt lead to increased scrutiny of other evangelists, and no doubt we'll discover more than one sinner amidst the self-proclaimed states.

With the end of the Reagan administration rapidly approaching, insiders are sure to try to capitalize by rushing into print with their "inside" looks at what really went on behind the scenes. In the quest for the best seller list, these books are sure to contain "ugly" incidents designed to garner headlines.

Finally, in any year we can count on that old reliable, human nature, to provide more than enough misdoings to fill any book. Fads may come and go, but millions and millions of us still fall prey to temptations large and

A LOOK TO SCANDAL IN 1988

small every hour of every day. We at the Paragon Project are waiting eagerly to collect those that inevitably bring the humiliation of public attention.

As in any other year, however, we realize we can't find everything. That's why we're once again inviting you readers to help us compile the *Scandal Annual—1988*. If you come across any major or minor scandal you think belongs in these pages, please send it to:

> THE SCANDAL ANNUAL
> c/o PaperJacks LTD.
> 210 Fifth Avenue
> New York, NY 10010

Any scandal that makes it into our 1988 book wins the reader who submits the story a free copy of *Scandal Annual—1988*.

FREE!!
BOOKS BY MAIL CATALOGUE

BOOKS BY MAIL will share with you our current bestselling books as well as hard to find specialty titles in areas that will match your interests. You will be updated on what's new in books at no cost to you. Just fill in the coupon below and discover the convenience of having books delivered to your home.

PLEASE ADD $1.00 TO COVER THE COST OF POSTAGE & HANDLING.

BOOKS BY MAIL
320 Steelcase Road E.,
Markham, Ontario L3R 2M1

IN THE U.S. -
210 5th Ave., 7th Floor
New York, N.Y., 10010

Please send Books By Mail catalogue to:

Name _____
(please print)

Address _____

City _____

Prov./State _____ P.C./Zip _____

(BBM1)